Criminal Camera

Criminal Camera

John Mackay

The Pentland Press Limited
Edinburgh • Cambridge • Durham • USA

© John Mackay 1996

First published in 1996 by
The Pentland Press Ltd.
1 Hutton Close
South Church
Bishop Auckland
Durham

All rights reserved.
Unauthorised duplication
contravenes existing laws.

British Library Cataloguing in Publication Data.
A Catalogue record for this book is available
from the British Library.

ISBN 1 85821 363 0

Typeset by CBS, Felixstowe, Suffolk
Printed and bound by Antony Rowe Ltd., Chippenham

To my wife Kay
A real partner for 52 years . . .

Foreword

The quick development of the romance between the young couple in the story and the stamina they show in walking and indeed climbing to such effect around Edinburgh, are all arranged simply to give the reader as many stories about the City as possible – especially those not found in the average guide book – and to lead them on to the 'home straight' for the thriller climax.

It may be of interest to note that certain details in the story are not fiction. The author had occasion once to have two tickets for a Festival concert and what worked so effectively in this tale did so for him – less the romance. The meeting with the two asking the way to Loch Lomond is also true, as was the German youth's climb. The author in his role as journalist, once interviewed the hall keeper at the Usher Hall who mentioned his meeting with the two world famous orchestra conductors. Also fact, a talk with the 'clock' apprentice on top of the Nelson Column. The lad forgot to lock the NO ADMISSION door – a 'key' incident when our hero and heroine become first involved with the criminal cameraman.

Chapter 1

When young Robert Hart spoke to the girl outside the Usher Hall in Edinburgh on the opening night of the Festival, he could not know that this would lead to their becoming involved later with criminals, in an episode sensational enough to warrant headlines in the national Press.

He had been told there were often last minute visitors hoping to get tickets that had been returned for the opening concert. Since he had been given two complimentary tickets from the advertising agency where he was employed and was fancy free at the moment, he had the idea of going to the Hall entrance before the concert began and waiting until some girl would be seen coming out of the doorway looking disappointed.

He would then ask if she would care for one of his tickets. When the situation actually happened and the girl was about to pass, he managed to blurt out, 'Excuse me miss, were you looking for a seat for this concert?'

June Ralston from London, newly arrived on holiday and staying with her maiden aunt, was well accustomed to the male approach. She looked at this blunt-nosed, healthy-looking specimen, so different from her recent boyfriend down south and said, 'Yes, have you one for sale?'

'For sale? No, I mean would you share a seat with me – I mean two seats, it's just that I've got these two tickets and I . . .'

'You mean you're sort of offering me the seat as a gift?'

'Yes, that's it.'

'Thank you very much,' smiled the girl, 'the white heather I was given yesterday has brought me luck.'

In silence they walked up the staircase by the memorial to Kathleen Ferrier, a star singer in the early years of the Festival, and on into the Hall.

'This is great,' said Miss Ralston as they settled into the comfortable seats in the Grand Tier. 'Thank you again,' and she began looking around the Hall . . .

He was nervous, never good at small talk, nor would he be with such a special-looking young lady beside him.

Robert began desperately searching his memory for a subject to talk about . . .

Racing through his mind were Usher Hall stories told him by his retired former journalist uncle. The fact that the Usher Hall was financially founded by Usher, the Distiller of world fame – as was Edinburgh's other concert hall – the McEwan Hall, by the equally famed Brewer of that name. No, too beery for a beginning. Would she be interested in the fact that this Grand Tier and the Gallery above were constructed on the cantilever principle? No supporting pillars, and since it was an innovation at the time, a squad of the Royal Scots Regiment were marched from the Castle prior to the hall's official opening before the First World War, to thump around on the seats of the two tiers unsupported by orthodox pillars, to test the safety of such a place for a capacity audience. That was told to his uncle by the sergeant-major in charge of the soldiers, now a pensioner accustomed to walking his dog on Calton hill. He had once talked to Robert's uncle of the 'goings on' he had witnessed on Calton hill in his time and – no, that definitely would not do. But there was one subject she would surely find of interest, the time his uncle had interviewed the hall-keeper about the famous orchestral conductors he had met. Sir Thomas Beecham? Yes, he would change his shirt during the interval sometimes, then the hall-keeper would give him a 'rub doon'. No, that wouldn't do either. Then Robert remembered something that *would* do, and turned to his companion.

'My uncle told me that he once interviewed the hall-keeper here and asked him who had been his favourite conductor of the many he had met with in his work in the hall. "Sir John Barbirolli was the one," said the hall-keeper, "every time he came with his orchestra he would ask how my wee daughter was getting on and ask to see her – our house was just across the lane from the side entrance – and then he would present her with a ten shilling note and say that's from your uncle John".'

'I can imagine Barbirolli doing that,' said June. 'Have you any other stories about Edinburgh and personalities of today?'

'Mostly about Edinburgh and not always guide book stuff. I work in an advertising agency and I got the job recently of getting material on the city and its history for a brochure we are doing.' Then Robert went off at a most unexpected tangent and blurted out to his own astonishment, 'I'm on holiday too, can I see you again?'

June's eyes momentarily widened in surprise at this sudden change of subject, then she nodded, smiled and said 'Yes.'

They grinned delightedly at each other, then the spell was broken by a burst of applause welcoming one more world-renowned conductor to the Festival.

Robert had never taken an interest in music of the symphony concert type, in fact this was his first experience of a live orchestra at full strength producing such a weight of sonorous sound to make an impression on him that he was likely never to forget. His companion of course may well have had something to do with this, her being there heightened his perception or something.

Enough it was for him to wait for the next tune to come in and since it was a piece by Brahms he was not too badly served with melody. Not that his mind was all on the concert.

Every now and then he would steal a sidelong glance at the profile next to him. Her frame of dark hair contrasted with the pale skin and even if Robert enjoyed no more than the briefest of glances he decided that here was 'class'. This 'copper-heided' young man was already her admirer.

They mingled with the audience in the foyer at the interval, he pointing out prominent notables of the Town – some with complimentaries like me, thought Robert – and probably in some instances with no more knowledge than he had of so called classical music.

They had their first chance to talk together then, and got as far as deciding they would meet tomorrow morning where they had first met, outside the main entrance of the Usher Hall.

The second part of the concert was similar to the first half, so far as stealing glances at a profile and waiting for the next tune to come along.

As they came out on to the pavement Robert said, 'I'll see you home.'

They walked along the gardens side of Princes Street, flanked on the left by traffic and shop fronts and on the right and below, by pop music from the gardens band stand; from on high, in opposition, came the sound of the massed Pipes and Drums from the Military Tattoo on the Castle Esplanade.

So to a quiet square of buildings off from Leith Walk and to the entrance of a series of flats where they stood in a small silence for a moment then shook hands.

"Til tomorrow,' said June.

'Tomorrow,' answered Robert and watched until the door closed; then off he went walking at speed to his lodging in the

Marchmont district. Not because he was in a hurry to get home; the unconsciously fast pace merely matched the speed with which thoughts of the evening events crowded through his mind, and what he would do tomorrow. He must remember to wear that new shirt he had got.

Chapter 2

Monday morning dawned bright with promise. Robert, having lain awake for what seemed to him most of the night, then slept profoundly towards morning, thanking his stars that he had set his alarm. He was at the entrance to the Usher Hall at the appointed time – but no sign of the lady. I've been 'stood up' he thought, or perhaps it's a woman's privilege to be late, as some moron must once have said. She seemed such a fine lass too, I'd never have thought . . .

June Ralston was flattered by the expression of delight on Robert's face as saw her coming up Lothian Road.

'Good morning, am I late?'

'No, no. Where would you like to go?'

'It's for you to say – you're the guide.'

'Well, I thought we could walk round the Castle rock by Johnston Terrace then either go down the Royal Mile or up to the Castle.'

'Right, lead on.'

Robert laughed. 'Lead on, eh? It makes me think of schooldays and a line from Macbeth: Lead on Macduff, and damned be he who first cries hold, enough! – or something like that.'

'We never did Macbeth, but we did Midsummer Night's Dream. We acted it too. I played Titania.'

'Then your opposite number was Oberon, right? There's a picture of the pair in the National Gallery here. We had a lad in our lot at school who pronounced Oberon as O'Brien – can you imagine it – O'Brien, king of the fairies.'

They both laughed and this brief daft Shakespearean interlude was enough to end any initial shyness between them.

Down they went to Castle Terrace and headed left to where Johnston Terrace began skirting the rock.

'This terrace is a Victorian engineering effort,' said Robert. 'Before it was built, the rock went sheer down into the Grassmarket below us and at this point I could tell you about two happenings at this place on the rock – well, three in fact, if the plaque on the grass slope inside the garden there at our back is included, for it marks the place where a Zeppelin bomb hit the slope, just missing the military barracks during the First World War. Another bomb landed in the Grassmarket in front of the Beehive Inn, making a large hole in the causeway. As a small boy, my grandfather remembers being taken down to see the damage next morning, and his main memory of that was the amount of broken glass all over the road.'

'Can I see this plaque?' asked June.

'No, at least not today, too much of a steep scramble in the long grass – but nothing like the scramble on this part of the rock above our heads. Once for real and once in fiction.'

Robert began his tale. 'Way back in the time of Robert the Bruce when that man set about winning the Scottish castles back from the occupying English, if you'll pardon the expression—'

June smiled, 'That's OK, my Mum's Scottish.'

'Glad to know that,' said Robert, and went on: 'One of Bruce's generals was Sir Thomas Randolph who got the job of recapturing the Castle of Edinburgh.'

By this time, the young couple were on the move round the terrace.

Robert continued. 'Randolph's problem, because he had

such a small force, was to try and surprise the enemy at a part of the wall on top of the rock which would be thought impregnable. At such a place there would be little chance of a patrolling guard.

'One night, Randolph and his men were discussing the project in a tavern in the Grassmarket, and one of the company, an "old sweat," thought he might have the solution. When he was a young soldier and stationed in the Castle, when of course it was Scots controlled, he had a girlfriend who lived in the Grassmarket. I doubt there were short leave passes in these early days of the fourteenth century, but anyway he got into the ploy of being absent without leave at night, just as often as he could contrive it. He chose a part of the rock above our heads here, where he had discovered what might be called a goat track all the way down from the top wall, not to this level of Johnston Terrace but all the way down to the Grassmarket.'

'And then?' enquired June.

'How do you mean?'

'Did he go all the way up again before morning?'

'Yes.'

'Gosh,' said that young lady. 'All the way down to be with his love, then all the way up before . . .'

'Before the medieval equivalent of the sergeant major would come into the barrack room where he, lover boy, not long sunk into an exhausted sleep would rudely be brought back to consciousness with the fourteenth century version of Wakey, wakey, rise and shine.'

'What a man, eh? True love indeed! But I'm interrupting you, Robert.'

'Yes, well on the chance that he, after all these years, could find the track again – and he did – what was then needed for the climb, was a rope ladder hooked at one end and their weapons muffled and slung over their shoulders to prevent the noise of metal scraping on the rock during the ascent. A few nights later, all was ready and the old boy led the way – and after a long struggle, reached the heights. The ladder was hooked on the ledge topping the wall. I reckon there would be a pause to listen if the noise had attracted the attention of any guard . . . then over the top, into the Castle, along to the barracks to the surprise of the temporary occupants mostly asleep and without a chance against the claymores.'

'What's a claymore?'

'It's English for the great sword, a two handed affair, you'll see some of them when we go to the Castle.'

'What a bloodthirsty lot! And what about your other story?'

'It will be very brief, you'll be glad to know – sure I'm not boring you?'

'Do I look bored? I'm interested, this is all new to me, no, go on then you can have a rest and I'll do a bit of talking.'

'This other one is fiction, Robert Louis Stevenson's novel *St Ives*.'

'Oh, my aunt is a Stevenson fan, she's got a lot of his stuff.'

'You ask her to let you have a go at this *St Ives*, even if you just read the bit about the main character's escape from the Castle. The hero's name is as used in the title. St Ives was a French prisoner of war who escaped down a rope at the same steep place we were looking at and these prisons where the French were kept have been reopened to the public. I'm not too clear on details for I've never read it all, but your aunt will know.'

'Oh yes, I'm sure she will. That reminds me, I'd better get this over now and hope I'm not going to spoil the rest of your day. Aunt says bring this young man to tea this afternoon – oh I'm really sorry, have I spoiled your day?'

'Och, I'm not good at that sort of thing, but I'd better get it over and done with. I could think of a different situation where

I could make my excuses.'

'Ah, in other words you're doing it for me.'

'That's it – like a lamb to the slaughter.'

'Bless you; she's not a dragon, you know, a bit stern at times but a real Scottish gem. You'll like her.'

'Aye, she'll want to vet me.' Robert took a deep breath of resignation and said, 'Here we are at the Castle Wynd stairs. You choose whether you want to climb them stairs or continue round to the end of the terrace and go down the Royal Mile.'

'Since I didn't climb to see the bomb plaque back there, I'm for the stairs.'

When they arrived on top they took a rest, lounging against the esplanade wall and Robert asked June about her office work in London. She explained how she got interested in orchestral music by trying concerts at the Proms in the Albert Hall to oblige a friend.

'A boyfriend?' asked Robert.

'Yes.'

'Do you – do you still . . .?'

'No, he was really too arty for me, but did me a good turn getting me to these concerts.'

A private smile to herself from June.

A secret hope stirring in Robert.

The Castle esplanade was not itself, shrunk as it was with all the stands for the spectators for the Tattoo, all empty until evening when a summer sunset would challenge the floodlighting of the Tattoo as to which would produce the most striking display.

They crossed the drawbridge and through the gateway flanked by the national heroes, King Robert the Bruce to the left, Sir William Wallace to the right.

They then began the way up into the Capital's historic fortress. Before they walked through the first archway, Robert drew attention to an inscription high on the wall at their left.

'Can you read that, June?'

'Yes, in part anyway. "In memory of Sir William Kirkcaldy of Grange . . . he held this Castle for Mary, Queen of Scots from 1568 to 1573 and after its honourable surrender, suffered death for devotion to her cause." Gosh, that's loyalty to Mary, eh? Why did he hold out all that time, do you know?'

'The power barons who ruled Scotland during the boyhood of Mary's son the future James VI, didn't want Mary, then exiled in England, to attempt a return to the throne. Religion came into it, as it often does in wars, and Kirkcaldy's holding of the Castle, for *he* wanted Mary back as Queen, ended when from the south came a force of Elizabeth's English artillery to augment the Scottish cannon of the power barons.

'They ringed the Castle for a month, eventually demolishing the main defence, the King David Tower, built in the mid fourteenth century,' Robert continued. 'The ruins of the Tower are under the Half-Moon Battery, that big curved wall I mentioned as we went up the esplanade. I like its old name. When it was built to replace the David Tower they called it The Great Half Bastion Round. But don't think I'm going on like this all the time, I never remember learning this at school. I had to swot it up for this brochure job.'

'Don't apologise, Robert. Holding the Castle for five years – how did they manage? I mean, they had to eat?'

'Aye, they ate. Kirkcaldy's men used to go into the town at night and down to the Port of Leith here to get supplies, they even began to make dud coins to trade with.'

Moving on, after that discussion, and passing under the archway of the Argyll Tower, the portcullis gate overhead still showing, they swung round the cobbled way to the summit of the rock.

June was intrigued to discover the little dog cemetery for

the regimental mascots; Robert was more intent on the gunnery on view.

So to the little Norman chapel of Saint Margaret's, the eleventh century Queen of Scots, and in contrast to view the great cannon, 'the auld murderess', Mons Meg.

'If you are ever at Norham Castle in the Borders,' said Robert, 'you can see what she did to the west door. Mons Meg was acquired by Cromwell, but returned on Sir Walter Scott's plea to George IV. The old cannon with a military cavalry escort, came back in style to the Castle.'

After queuing for a brief glimpse of the Regalia in Crown Square, June and Robert found an empty seat outside.

'That crown you just saw as the centre-piece of the Regalia,' remarked Robert, 'has quite a story – or have you had enough?'

'As I said before, I'm interested.'

'Right, I'll make it brief. Cromwell, having pinched Mons Meg, was liable to do the same with the Regalia, being without the Scots regard for such things. So, before he got the length of Edinburgh, the Regalia was taken to Dunnottar castle on the coast south of Aberdeen and put in charge of the governor of that citadel, a very sparsely garrisoned place, too. In time, Cromwell's soldiers were in the area and it was a matter of days before they would take the castle of Dunnottar. In fact a few were already on guard duty on the cliff top opposite Dunnottar which happens to be almost isolated from the mainland, and nearly circled by the coastal seas.

'It happened,' Robert continued, 'that the minister's wife to the kirk of Kinneff a few miles down the coast, came up at intervals to collect cloth spun by the governor's wife to help her pass the weary hours within the castle. Imagine it now. Here comes the minister's wife on her old horse. The Cromwellian Roundhead nods to her as she dismounts and leads her horse down the path to the shore and up to the castle gate. After a while up she comes again leading her mount and carrying a bale of cloth. When she reaches the top of the cliff, the soldier obligingly helps her on to the saddle and then sets the bale athwart the saddle front firmly and off she goes the seven miles down the cliff-top path to Kinneff.'

'I can guess what happened in the castle,' smiled June.

'Aye, well maybe not exactly, for inside the bale of cloth there was the Sword of State presented to King James IV by the Pope of that time in the early 1500s along with the Sceptre but—'

'And the Crown?'

'But the Crown wasn't – it was tied round her waist and hidden under the voluminous skirts of the fashion then.'

'Does your story have a happy ending?'

'It does. Some versions have it that the minister's wife had her little maid with her, but what is fact is that the minister buried the Crown under the stone paving in front of the pulpit and there it remained until it was returned to the Castle here.'

'Some story – it would make a good film, eh?'

'Aye, and so would a few other stories around this area, but we must cross to the Scottish National War Memorial, now you've had a rest.'

From all they saw in the Castle, Robert got the impression that June would remember most the brief visit to the National Memorial – not that she said much apart from whispering as they walked the Hall of Honour – 'It's lovely to see stained glass that lets the daylight through . . .'

The Banqueting Hall impressed too. 'You'll see something like that when we go down the Royal Mile – the inside of the Parliament Hall – something a lot of tourists miss. To change the subject, would you like an early lunch?'

'Yes, please.'

'Just a bit too early for the Castle restaurant but by the time we get to the High Street part of the Mile, it should be about midday. We'll miss the one o'clock gun fired here but I expect you'll be back to the Castle with your aunt during your holiday and you can tell her all about the place, now that you are so well informed.'

June laughed. 'Anyhow I bet I'll remember most of your stories. Who fires this gun?'

'From the Royal Observatory at the south of the City on Blackford Hill an electrical impulse is sent to the electrically controlled clock beside the gun on the dot of one o'clock. That triggers off the bang.'

'And it's fired every day?'

'Every week day. Sunday is a day of rest, even for the gun. In Victorian times a local businessman, on a trip to Paris had seen something similar operating as a midday gun and when he came back here suggested that Edinburgh should have something like that too. I think the one he saw in Paris may have been a later version of the story I found when rummaging in the local library. I got a photocopy of a newspaper cutting – I've got it somewhere here,' and he took out an old and fat wallet. After a bit of sifting through he handed June the cutting saying, 'Read that.'

They stopped by one of the Castle seats and June read: 'In the gardens of the Palais Royal, there is a little brass cannon, known as *le petit canon* which was invented by an eighteenth century clockmaker to fire automatically on the stroke of midday. The ingenious mechanism works by means of a large magnifying glass, adjusted to concentrate the rays of sunlight on a powder generator when the sun is exactly at the zenith.'

'Of course, on cloudy days,' said Robert, 'it would be silent, not like this one here. When it was first tried out it had old ladies parading in Princes Street, nearly jumping out of their skins as the authorities fired the gun at all times of the day.

They were settling on the best position for it in the Castle.'

They resumed their downward stroll towards the arched Argyll Tower.

'You said it was fired electrically – but surely someone is in charge?'

'Oh aye, always a retired artillery man who loads the shell. He's responsible for getting the ammunition ready when there's a salute of guns from the Battery, like when some important person is coming by sea to visit the Capital and arriving at the Port of Leith. As their ship sails up the Firth, so the salute begins, a twenty-one gun salute if it's Royalty. Mentioning the old boy who loads the one o'clock gun, when he was in the army in the last World War, he was stationed on Inchkeith, the island in the middle of the Firth. A merchant ship, one of ours, was seen approaching the submarine barrier and the order was given to fire a shot, a dummy one, across her bows to let her know she was coming along the wrong channel for shipping. The shell, being much lighter than one with a full load of explosive, acted in the same way as when a flat stone is skimmed across water, and went bouncing across the waves and into the brick wall near a kitchen where a housewife was preparing lunch.'

'Was she hurt?'

'No, the woman, as they found out later, when the Leith officials complained of gunnery practices in the wrong direction, although very surprised and shocked, did not suffer any damage, only the wall alongside.'

As they walked under the Argyll Tower, June asked, 'Why did you call this a State prison?'

'That's where all the big shots were held before execution – including a Duke of Argyll. Now, although you are the one for music, June, I'm a bit for pictures and although I'm not sure about this, I've seen a reproduction of a famous painting called

"Argyll's Last Sleep" and I have the idea that maybe it showed him in there on the night before his execution.*

'One story I did find recently is about a minor character put in there before he featured in a procession staged to warn any other would-be terrorist that crime doesn't pay. But I'll tell you about that at lunch – you've had enough crime this morning to keep you going for a while.'

They both laughed. No way could they be aware that in the coming afternoon of this eventful day for them, a first hint of crime eventually to involve June and Robert, was being arranged by Fate.

Meantime they were coming to top end of the Royal Mile, and in the Lawnmarket, Robert pointed across to a corner building, Deacon Brodie's Tavern, and asked, 'Would this tavern in the town suit?'

'Yes, thank you.'

'And you'll take a wee drink first? And I'll tell you about wee Mr Watt.'

They settled down in an upstairs room and Robert said, 'Something tells me it would be typical of you to ask who Deacon Brodie was?'

June grinned. 'I was about to ask.'

'He'll have to wait. There's enough about that character to make a book by itself. I'll tell you about him – or at least a bit

---

* The painting *The Last Sleep of Argyll* by E.M. Ward is in the collection of Salford Art Gallery, Manchester.

The Marquis of Argyll, an adherent of the Scottish Covenanters, was tried in the reign of Charles II for treason and executed by the 'Maiden', a guillotine style of instrument (now on view in the Museum of Antiquities in Queen Street).

On the day of execution Argyll was served dinner by his own men before taking his last sleep. At the execution in the High Street he insisted that the block be properly levelled by a carpenter before he would place his head on it.

about him – later. No, he wasn't a church deacon, he was a Deacon of the Wrights, in his case, a sort of head man in the craft of carpentry. There's a cabinet made by him once acquired by Robert Louis Stevenson who some say took Brodie as his inspiration for Dr Jekyll and Mr Hyde. It's on show in the Lady Stair's House museum just up the Lawnmarket from here. But now for wee Mr Watt.

'He was a wine merchant in the town, and a leader of The Friends of the People, a collection of fanatics with copy-cat ideas from the French Revolution then recently successfully concluded. Yes, they had correspondence with Paris and Dublin too, asking for advice.

'This local lot,' Robert continued, 'held secret meetings in comparative safety among the darkness of the crowds at the cockfights in the Grassmarket and they had big ideas. A fire was to be raised in the High Street one night which meant that soldiers stationed in the Castle would come down to attend to keeping it under control and then extinguish it, which was part of their duties at that time. It was planned that as they returned to the Castle, they would be confronted by an armed body of the "Friends" who would incite them to mutiny. Then a letter was to be sent to King George II telling him to agree to their proposals or *take the consequences* – aye, what a nerve, eh?

'They might have got away with at least part of this daft scheme except that Sheriff officers, happening to include Watt's premises in search for an alleged bankrupt's goods known to be hidden somewhere in the district, came across a collection of pikes, these long spears that seem always to be associated with Revolution and, also typical, a machine set to print mutinous leaflets.

'Later the officers found that two blacksmiths had been given an order to supply 4000 of these pikes. Watt was out of luck. He was arrested.'

June asked, 'And no one else arrested?'

'Oh yes, and among them his second in command, a goldsmith called Dowie who at least got off with his life, being transported to the Colonies. But Watt got the complete works. His finish was staged in a kind of medieval style. He was brought in procession from the Argyll Tower in a cart painted black and drawn by a white horse, flanked by the Town Guard and a detachment of a Highland regiment from the Castle. They came in procession to the sound of The Dead March – a memorable scene for the crowds packing the Lawnmarket and the head of the High Street – the Edinburgh folk always relished a good hanging.'

'So this procession passed just outside here, Robert?'

'Aye, in 1794. And when you think of it, all happening just fifty years before that church spire at the top of the Lawnmarket was built. And there's a grand climax. After he was hanged at the scaffold across there by St Giles, the body was laid on the scaffold platform for a while, then the executioner reappeared carrying a long handled axe. When it dawned on the crowd what was going to happen next, those near the scaffold began fighting their way back out from the mob. A hanging was acceptable, but this was too savage even for the Edinburgh citizens of that time.'

June was aware an American couple at the next table had gone quiet as Robert ended with, 'The axe swung – and in the traditional way of the French Revolution which had inspired Mr Watt, his head was held on high to the cry "Behold the head of the traitor!"'

Robert looked solemnly at June then grinned and said, 'And here's the lass with the menu, I hope you have a good appetite.'

Chapter 3

After lunch, a slow walk down Bank Street to the Mound and in by the gardens gate to the slope above the railway, where they found a seat on the grass and away from the crowd below. When they did talk, it was not about Edinburgh, but about themselves and their hopes for the future.

Harsh reality returned on realising that time had passed like a dream and June's aunt was formidably awaiting in the wings.

'I hope,' growled Robert, 'there won't be yon chocolate eclair things and stuff I can't handle easy; being ill at ease and handling a chocolate eclair at the same time means trouble.'

'No, no, no I told her we would be having lunch early probably, and we had. Thank you again, in spite of the hangman, so, just a cup of tea. She's an expert with home made shortbread fingers though.'

'Maybe. Och well, let's go, June, and wish me luck.'

June's aunt, Miss Macower, had been a faithful secretary to a distinguished lawyer in Edinburgh for many years and on her retirement was financially rewarded to an extent that ensured a comfortable life as a senior citizen in the quiet square off Leith Walk where the two had now arrived.

'Here we are, auntie. This is Robert, Robert Hart, my aunt, Miss Macower.'

'Good afternoon, Mr Hart.' A very appraising look followed. 'I'm going to be "with it" as they seem to say nowadays and call you Robert, Heart of Midlothian, eh? Explain that to June while I go and make a dish o' tea.'

'It's a local football club, spelt H.E.A.R.T and also *The Heart of Midlothian* is a novel by Sir Walter Scott and there's a heart-shaped pattern in stones outside St Giles' where the Tolbooth prison used to be.'

A pause . . . Robert's recent role as a City tour lecturer was about to start off again, partly through nervousness until he wisely decided that this was the last place to be going on like he had before. Miss Macower soon arrived with a large laden tray. After the business of serving tea, June said, 'Robert was telling me this morning about St Ives and his escaping from the Castle and I said you would know.'

'Aye, he escaped for he was aiming for Swanston village in the Pentland Hills south of the city. The lass in the story who is called Flora, stayed with an elderly relative there and it was a habit of the time for visitors to the Castle to inspect and buy the work of the French prisoners, with their carvings set out on the pavement in front of their quarters. Some good work was done, model sailing ships made from bones and the like, and of course, romance is hinted at,' and Miss Macower smiled at Robert who wished he could disappear temporarily. She continued, 'One day, St Ives, who had been attracted by the youthful Flora, asks where she lives and she points out where smoke is rising from a cottage chimney in a fold of the Pentlands.' Miss Macower looked again at Robert. 'Yes, I know that it's doubtful if smoke at Swanston could be seen from the Castle, just a wee bit of artist's licence from Stevenson, eh?'

'Unless,' suggested Robert, 'it was a clearer atmosphere then and Edinburgh would be smaller at that time.'

'That's true – have another shortbread. But the crafty lad, St Ives, said to Flora when she had managed to steer away from her elderly chaperone, that he had asked her to point out her house, so that he knew of at least one home where there was a friend in this, to him, foreign land. In fact he was making sure that if he escaped, there was maybe a place of refuge at hand.'

'And then, auntie?'

'I'll leave it there in case you read the story some time, but I'll tell you that he gets to the cottage and then sent on his way south in the company of an old drover who knew the byways that would give St Ives a better chance of avoiding arrest. There's one bit in that part of the story that aye makes me smile – when St Ives and the drover get on their way walking a moorland track in the Borders, a gentleman on horseback coming from the south, stops to have a word with the drover. After he rides on St Ives asks, "Who was that?" Says the drover, "That was the Shirra, man, awbody kens the Shirra".'

Robert grinned. 'I like that – Sir Walter Scott, Sheriff of Selkirk making an appearance in fiction.'

'That Swanston,' continued Miss Macower, 'I aye feel sorry for Stevenson when he penned that poem when he was as you might say, exiled in Samoa and thinking of Swanston where his parents had the cottage and his beloved Pentland Hills. It goes something like this:

> "The tropics vanish and meseems that I,
> From steep Caerketton or topmost Allermuir dreaming,
>   gaze again
> Far set in fields and woods the Town I see, spring gallant
>   from the shallows of her smoke,
> Cragged spired and turreted, her virgin fort beflagged."

There's more, but that's the kind of gist of it.'

Robert knew that the castle was not virgin, having been taken by the English more than once but shied away from bringing up the particular word in this company, nor look as if he was catching RLS out again.

And surely the following put the accolade of approval on Robert when Miss Macower said, 'With such weather as we're having Robert, you should take June to Swanston one day – and even climb Caerketton.'

'I'd like to do that,' volunteered Robert, feeling more and more at home in this elderly character's company.

'I've got another story connected with a house very near to here that might interest you two.'

They both laughed and June said, 'Yes, make Robert the audience for a change – he's due a rest from lecturing anyway.'

'Just beyond the corner of this Square,' began Miss Macower, 'there's Gayfield House, a Georgian mansion, still impressive although no longer surrounded by its own grounds as it was before the town spread as far as this.

'One early morning, towards the end of the eighteenth century, a young man could have been seen leaving the house and mounting his horse to head west at the gallop. The young man was Thomas Graham, descended from the Dukes of Montrose. When he was twenty-seven he married Mary Shaw, ten years his junior. Mary's father, the 9th Baron Cathcart, had retired as Ambassador to the Court of Empress Catherine of Russia in 1771 and settled at the family home at Shaw Park near Alloa.

'Graham and his wife had arrived the previous evening as guests at Gayfield House to attend a Ball in the Assembly Rooms in George Street the next day and she had discovered that she had forgotten to take her jewel case with her when their luggage was brought in from the pack horse that had accompanied them on their journey from their home near Methven in Perthshire.'

'Why was he off at the gallop?' asked June.

'You may well ask – to get the jewel case, see?'

'But how,' persisted June, 'if the Ball was that night and he had to—?'

'A relay of horses?' suggested Robert.

'Just that,' said Miss Macower. 'And he'd have a rest when he crossed the Forth at Queensferry, then another fresh mount and off again Methven way; an about-turn, and back in time for his young wife to dress for the Ball – and him too of course for he'd be gey "horsey" after all that.'

'There's devotion for you eh?' commented June, and added, 'If she was only seventeen how could she have all these jewels and—?'

'Wedding presents too, wouldn't you say?' interrupted the aunt. 'But I don't think that was mentioned anywhere. What is more to the point is that the poor lass was soon discovered to be suffering from tuberculosis. They had been staying in London just after their marriage at a house belonging to her father, but soon moved north to the Graham family home near Methven, for both liked best the country life, she herself being a good horsewoman.'

'That must have been some time after the Ball in Edinburgh?' asked June.

'Oh yes. Sadly her condition deteriorated and her husband decided they should go on a long tour of France and Spain in the hope that the warmer lands in the south might restore her to better health and be kinder to her delicate beauty which had already been portrayed by Gainsborough in the second year of their marriage. This masterwork, entitled, "The Hon. Mrs Graham", was said by the artist himself to be "the very completest of pictures".'

Then Miss Macower introduced her punchline, 'And you can judge for yourself for the painting is in the National Gallery here at the Mound, gifted to the people of Scotland on condition that it never leaves the country.'

Robert knew the picture but not the story behind it and was about to say so, when Miss Macower added, 'I know of a young man who goes to the Gallery at times, just to see the painting – I think he's in love with her.'

Robert decided then not to say anything except to agree that he would take June some time to see the Gainsborough. She then enquired, 'Is that the end of your story about Mrs Graham, auntie?'

'No, indeed, but are you not tired of this auld wife rambling on, eh? Am I not keeping you from some show or something you've planned, for you know June, you'll have to make some duty calls with me on other relatives here which will mean that some days you won't have Robert as escort.'

Said Robert, 'June and I thought we'd try one of the Fringe shows later, so there's no hurry.'

'Aye,' remarked their hostess, 'I think we take pot luck with some of these Fringe affairs – either finding a performance that eventually finishes up in the West End of London with one or two of the cast on the first steps to becoming big names in the theatre – or a show which you decide to leave at the first interval and get out to the fresh air. Certainly the Fringe, and oh, I wish they wouldna stick their posters all over the place, then leave them as half torn relics after the Festival for us townsfolk to suffer the sight o', – but as I was saying, certainly the Fringe has the advantage of being good material for the media, being more sensational and whiles more gimmicky than the official concerts etc. But here's me rantin' on, forgetting that as they say, youth must have its fling, but now I'll get back to finish my story. There's not much more. They did a second tour in 1792 and this promised better for Mary Graham. Her condition seemed to improve for some time, but when they arrived in Nice she collapsed and was kept in bed for two days. Once again, a revival of her condition and her husband much relieved, it was arranged that they go on a sea tour along the coast in the month of June.

A few days later Thomas Graham went ashore to a village for supplies and when he returned to the little vessel his young wife was dead.

'Then began the terrible journey home to Scotland,' continued Miss Macower, 'first by boat on a canal heading for Bordeaux. Near Toulouse, they were stopped by a drunken mob of revolutionaries, the French Revolution apparently getting into its stride. They boarded the boat – and the ultimate horror! – they insisted on opening the coffin, suspecting smuggled goods inside. While some held back the enraged husband with difficulty, others forced off the lid of the coffin. The disclosure seemed almost to sober the gang and poor Graham was allowed on his way.'

'Oh that lot were horrible, that was awful,' said June.

'Aye, anyway, that was the last Graham saw of any revolutionaries; in time, and it must have been a wearying time, they arrived home.

'But Graham could never forget that violation and nursed a hatred of the French Revolution and all it stood for, turning him from a country-loving squire, into a military-minded man intent on revenge.

'He sold part of the Balgowan family estate and raised the "Balgowan Green Breeks", later to be linked with "The Cameronians (Scottish Rifles)" and in time to become second in command to the Duke of Wellington.'

'Maybe he was at the battle of Waterloo,' suggested Robert and Miss Macower agreed that that was very likely.

'What a story – poor Mary,' sighed June. 'And was she buried in the grounds of their home or was there a church?'

'Graham had a mausoleum built in the kirk grounds near Methven, for his young wife. I've visited it, a sad kind of place.

Her best memorial is surely that lovely Gainsborough, begun when she was just eighteen.'

Chapter 4

Next day, Tuesday, June spent with her aunt. Meeting Robert again on Wednesday morning at their usual rendezvous she was surprised to find that it seemed a long time since she had last seen him.

After going into the National Gallery to see 'The Hon. Mrs Graham', and an early lunch at the Abbotsford in Rose Street, they were heading for the Royal Mile, when, nearing the east end of Princes Street, June caught sight of the tall column on Calton hill and asked what it was.

'A monument to Nelson – Admiral Lord Nelson, winner of the Battle of Trafalgar, and put up by a grateful nation.'

'Could we get to the top of that?'

'We could. You want to go up there instead of to the Royal Mile?'

'It's such a clear day, won't there be good views from up top?'

'There sure will be.'

'Then let's go.'

That last brief sentence marked the prelude to a complete upheaval of their holiday when, in the following week, if not before, Robert Hart had to decide whether or not to contact the Police in a situation fraught with real danger to the young couple, with enough excitement for them to warrant the closing days of their holiday time becoming a real thriller.

They walked up Waterloo Place, that remarkable extension

of the line of Princes Street, remarkable in its construction in that a great swathe was cut out through the ancient Calton cemetery to make way for this fine Georgian street, the macabre underground contents being re-interred in the Regent Road burial ground further east.

June and Robert took the short flight of steps on the left leading on to the Hill, passing a wrought iron gate with the lettering, 'Rock House', once the home and studio of David Octavius Hill, an artist of the Royal Scottish Academy, but also happening to be a pioneer of photography in the days when the sitter had to try and sit still for two minutes in bright sunlight before any image could appear within the primitive camera of the time.

On top of the hill, first to a seat, he had to explain that there was no escalator – there were one hundred and forty-five steps to the top. Did she still want to go? She did.

Inside the base of the column Robert showed June the model of Nelson's ship *Victory*, but what intrigued her more was the facsimile of a letter headed, 'On board *Victory*' and beginning, 'My dear and beloved Emma' . . .

When they were nearing the top, a sound like muted thunder rumbled down the stairway.

June, wild-eyed, looked a question to her companion.

'Sorry, that will be the time ball coming down the shaft.'

The ball is raised to the top a few minutes before one o'clock, now only operated as a tradition – a memory of the old seafaring days when mariners out on the Firth of Forth would train their telescopes on the ball and, as it dropped at one o'clock, check their timepieces.

As they arrived at the top balcony, at least the ultimate one for visitors, a youth came out of the door marked NO ADMISSION leading to the higher short flight of stairs in the part of the column housing the shaft of the time ball.

This lad was flattered to explain to them his job as apprentice in the firm who looked after all the public clocks in the city. He had come up to check the time-ball mechanism.

When the clock caretaker had clattered off downstairs and they had the balcony to themselves, June said, 'Some view, and isn't it clear. I think I see aunt's window, and look at the hills across the river.'

It made a panorama through 360 degrees. Looking along Princes Street like a giant broadsword blade separating the Old Town from the New and with the viewer beginning clockwise, could be seen, from that prospect, a glimpse of the Forth Rail and Road bridges then north to the hills of Fife and continuing by the islands on the river – Inchcolm, 'The Iona of the East', Inchkeith and round to the bird sanctuary of the Isle of May on the horizon to nearer on that line in East Lothian, Berwick Law, the Bass Rock and Traprain Law leading the eye south – east to Arthur's Seat then down below, the Palace of Holyroodhouse at the foot of the Royal Mile, and so up that ridge of the Old Town by the crown steeple of St Giles with the Pentland Hills as background, to the Castle and back to Princes Street with the rotunda-style memorial to Professor Dugald Stewart, friend of Robert Burns in the immediate foreground.

The burial ground above Waterloo Place is dominated by a tall obelisk raised to the 'Chartist Martyrs' who were tried in 1793 for 'speaking words tending to excite discord between King and People' and sentenced to transportation for life (friends of Mr Watt?). Nearby the obelisk stood the statue of President Abraham Lincoln also serving as a memorial to the Scots-American soldiers who fought in the Civil War.

Robert said, 'I'm looking to see if the cone of Ben Lomond shows, but I don't think so, it can be seen from the top of Arthur's Seat though, if you know where to look.'

He laughed and added, 'Have you heard of the song the

Bonny Banks of Loch Lomond?'

'Yes, my Mum knows it.'

'Aye, well this happened to me recently. I was walking along Princes Street when I was stopped in my tracks by a deep voice belonging to one of two gentlemen.

"Parm me, which way to Lack Lomond?" I was asked.

'Oh em, if you continue along to the end of this street and turn left, there's a bus station which—'

"We garra car."

'Ah well, do a U turn and continue on the line of Princes Street further west until you come to two roads with a public clock in the middle. Take the right hand road and that's on the way to Glasgow where you can enquire again.'

"Is it a big siddy?'

'Yes, Glasgow is one of the biggest—'

"Nah, nah, Lack Lomond, is Lack Lomond a big siddy?"

'A big – Loch Lomond is water, a loch, a lake, famous Scottish loch.'

"Aw! Thanks all the same."

'And off they went,' concluded Robert. 'I suppose, heading for the bonny banks, or would it be worth their while? I began to wonder you see, if they were crooks, then what a disappointment it must have been for them to discover that the banks were not the kind in their minds.'

'I expect lots of tourists get mixed up too with dates in history, especially if they're dashing around all over the place,' said June.

'Oh aye, like the lady who remarked, "How Mary Queen of Scots chose to live so far away from the Princes Street shops I'll never understand – what woman in her senses would stay in a so called Palace at Holyrood near all these breweries".'

June laughed. 'I know one thing about Holyrood that may be news even to you but I'll keep it until we get there,' and she refused to satisfy Robert's curiosity who said, 'OK, just one item more before we go down: see that cannon on the hill below us, it's an antique, at least the bronze barrel is. When the Spaniards were colonising out west, the Portuguese were doing the same in the Far East. I think both must have had some connection with the cannon for both Spanish and Portuguese heraldic arms are shown.

'The Burmese got into these wars and captured the cannon – the capture is recorded in Burmese script on the side of the barrel. Then the British got into the act in their campaigns out east and in time this ancient piece of artillery was exhibited in one of the great Victorian exhibitions before being presented to Edinburgh.'

'It sure got around, as they say.'

'It sure did – hey, look at this! The clock boy didn't lock the no admission door. See? There's no handle, just the keyhole, must remember to tell the ticket woman when we get downstairs.'

Robert put a finger into the keyhole and the door swung outwards disclosing a small stairway circling a cog-wheeled metal column leading to the topmost balcony where the time-ball now rested.

'Let's go up,' suggested Robert.

'Not allowed.'

'Och come on, there's nobody to stop us and you can say you got to where no other visitor has been.'

'Just for a minute then,' said June, looking fastidiously into the dusty, oily gloom of the small circular room, before following Robert up the short flight of stairs.

There was just room up there for them and the time-ball, huge in close-up.

'What about taking it home as a souvenir?' grinned Robert, then his expression changed, and he whispered, 'Someone is coming up the main stair, we'd better get down, easy now, let me help you.'

A now apprehensive young lady and a keenly listening young man stood at the inner side of the NO ADMISSION door.

'Too late to chance going out,' he whispered again, as the sound of footsteps grew ever louder in the echoing twisting stairway . . .

More whispering. 'It seems there's more than one lot of footsteps, let's hope they'll just go round the balcony and then down again.'

But 'they' stayed longer than was comfortable for the couple behind the NO ADMISSION door while Robert put a finger into the keyhole again, keeping his arm at full-stretch to ensure that the door to all appearances stayed shut. They heard the sound of footsteps arriving on to the balcony and of someone somewhat 'out of puff'. The footsteps faded as they went round to the other side of the balcony then returned and a whining Cockney voice said, 'Why did we have to come up here in this flaming bloody heat anyway?'

'Because, Syd,' answered a breathless, more elderly and faintly pompous voice, 'although I'm an old fashioned cameraman now – I shudder at the sight of these young press ladies with a lens about as big as themselves – I'm still a good photographer and even under the present unusual circumstances, cannot resist recording subject matter like the prospect from this viewpoint. I'm quite sure it will be of use later, always assuming I'll be a free man after Thursday next week.'

If the listeners could have seen him then, they would have noticed an expression of unease crawl across his florid face.

Then he continued on a more cheerful note, 'But why shouldn't we be free after next Thursday, eh? If there's a hitch, we play it straight; if things go according to plan, the earliest they could find out would be the Friday, by which time we'll have vanished from the scene, in fact they may never find out for a time. All we've got to do is keep our nerve at the climax. And think of the lovely money, Syd, that's coming our way.'

In the silence that followed, the click of a camera shutter was heard once or twice. Then the photographer again, 'Remember Syd, get that phrase into your head. Remember to wait until I . . .'

The rest of the sentence was lost as the strange duo moved to the other side of the balcony. June raised her eyebrows and nodded to the door. Robert shook his head and signed that they should wait until the two went down the stairway again. Robert was much relieved that they hadn't to wait too long, and before the cameraman and his companions began the descent of the twisting stairway, they heard the older man say, 'Whatever happens, keep the lid very steady and when I say "*Note the reflector gentlemen,*" you make your move on the word *gentlemen* – we've got it down to 15 seconds – I want it down to 10. Remember now, remember when I say the word . . .'

'OK,' breathed Robert, 'but let's wait a bit, can you imagine what they'd think if they heard footsteps following them down from on high.'

'We'll keep back from the balcony railing, they might just look up.'

'Aye, that's them making for the car park, that old red Herald is theirs. Aye, it is. Can you make out the registration number, June? No, nor me. Anyway, let's stay up here on the chance that we see the car going down Waterloo Place and that might give us an idea which way they are heading.'

They went round the balcony and faced towards Princes Street.

Down came the red Herald in Waterloo Place but then swung round right to Leith Street.

'Wait now,' said Robert with a touch of excitement in his voice, 'See if it reappears in that gap showing in Leith Walk.'

They turned to the north facing part of the balcony but no red car reappeared. 'That means they have either gone down Broughton Street way or one of the other openings before the square where your aunt lives.'

'What if they're not staying in Edinburgh?' added June. And on that unhelpful note they looked solemnly at each other.

Robert said, 'All we know is that a week tomorrow there's something funny going to happen, probably in Edinburgh, and I don't mean funny ha ha either.'

Another solemn look.

This, thought Robert, is where I kiss her and did just that. June pressed her cheek against his. Robert Hart was now a very happy young man.

Without a word they went slowly downstairs. They forgot to tell the attendant about the unlocked door. They forgot to look at the ancient cannon. They crossed to one of the empty seats by the Observatory wall and sat down.

After sunning themselves for a while, they wandered down the hill on its eastern side and found themselves at the end of Regent Terrace with Leith Walk at their left.

'Och, why have we got ourselves here?' muttered Robert. 'We should have gone down to Waterloo Place again and up to the Royal Mile – or do we want the Royal Mile today?'

June shook her head. 'Not in the mood now – let's just wander, eh?'

Robert agreed. They walked towards Leith Walk and crossed the busy thoroughfare to the north side of York Place.

Across from them, number 47 marked the one time home of Alexander Nasmyth, the artist friend of Robert Burns and painter of the best known portrait of Scotland's national poet. At number 47 Nasmyth also had his studio and his art classes whose pupils included his family one of whom, son James, born in 1808, became a renowned engineer whose drawing ability nurtured in his father's art class served him well in the designing of his inventions including that formidable mechanical giant, the steam hammer.

Robert pointed to the stone-carved artists's palette on the facade of number 32. 'Sir Henry Raeburn's house once, and his studio. You saw his version of what a Highland chief should look like in the National Gallery.' June's guide then pointed to the National Portrait Gallery and Museum of Antiquities at the end of Queen Street. 'Worth a visit too, but not for a day like this. No, let's get into the real "New Town" where, as someone once told me, it's laid down that all metal work be painted black, all window frames painted white, but the colours of the outer doors left to the discretion of the owners.'

They turned down to Dublin Street and took the first opening left, pacing the gentle curve of Abercrombie Place to cross into Heriot Row.

In the gardens to the left, the privileged key-owners were arranged in picnic pattern or sun bathing and children invented ball games.

Here was an Edinburgh of grace and space, far removed from the dark confines of the 'Old Town' as former inhabitants of the Royal Mile found when they moved here in the eighteenth and nineteenth centuries.

'There's a small round pond in the gardens said to be where the boy Stevenson got his first idea, developed in later life, for his famous tale *Treasure Island*,' said Robert. Further along the row and with a fine sense of timing he nodded at the front door of number 17 where a metal plate at the base of the old street lantern quoted from RLS's *Child's Garden of Verses*':

'For we are very lucky with a lamp before our door' his boyhood memory of watching from the upstairs room of this, his parents' house, for the approach of 'Leerie' the lamplighter.

At the end of Heriot Row they turned left up to Queen Street and then right, up North Castle Street. Robert pointing out a bust of Sir Walter Scott above the doorway of number 39 said, 'That's business premises now, but Scott's home for many years.'

Scott would leave the Law Courts in the High Street and after dining, often devote the rest of the evening writing at his desk. That was why when some young lawyers were having one of their parties in a top flat at the corner of George Street they could look down to a half-curtained window at the rear of number 39 North Castle Street, to wonder at what they called 'the moving hand' – the hand holding the pen of the creator of the Waverley novels.

'Now for some tea. You choose. Restaurant or the open air sunshaded place in Princes Street gardens.'

'The open air,' said that young lady, looking forward to sitting down.

Refreshed by the tea, they were on the move again out to King's Stables Road, the stables referring to those of medieval times and where also jousting tournaments took place.

So under the tunnel below Johnston Terrace to the west end of the Grassmarket. Robert, with a questioning eyebrow pointed across to the flight of steps known as the Vennel.

'Oh no,' sighed June, 'what a terrible town this, for stairs.'

'Aye, but you'll find it worthwhile when we get to the top for you'll see a view of, to give it its proper title – 'The Castle of Edinburgh' – which knocks all other views of the castle for six.'

She, having got to the top, agreed. The eye, looking down the narrow chasm of The Vennel, crosses the broad way of the

Grassmarket then travels upwards on the rock that Lord Randolph and his men climbed and St Ives had spun down, all crowned by the Banqueting Hall; in between that and the Half-Moon Battery, the historic fortress walls masking the Royal apartments where Mary Queen of Scots gave birth to her son James, the future first monarch to reign over Britain.

Turning their backs at last on the prospect, and with the old town wall on their left, they arrived in Lauriston and headed east, passing the gateway to George Heriot's School, a gateway deserving more than a brief glance and worthy of the architectural splendour of the main building seen up the drive.

The school was founded by George Heriot, goldsmith to James VI (referred to above) but occupied in the first instance as a hospital and barracks by Oliver Cromwell's troops during his attempted subjugation of Royal Scotland, illustrating his flair for disregarding the planned use of buildings elsewhere in this country.

Down now, on the Meadow Walk with the rear of the buildings of George Square on their left. One of the windows there once had a mirror fixed so that the young Walter Scott when ill in bed could pass his time watching the passers by on this same walk.

Robert said, 'We're in the University world now,' as he guided her through a passageway into the square itself and down to number 25, the boyhood home of Scott who, when active, was something of an irritation to the lady of the house next door since 'little Wattie' was forever paying her informal visits. When active too in his youth, he took part in this area of the city in the 'Town versus Gown' scuffles.

In contrast to the rest of this very Georgian Square the towers of the new buildings of the University of Edinburgh had been designed by a local lad who made good, Sir Basil Spence, architect, among much else, of the new Coventry Cathedral.

The wandering two now found themselves in the busy street projecting from the North & South Bridge roadways, and Robert armed June onto a bus for a well earned rest, passing Surgeons Hall and the magnificent façade of the domed older University building fronting the 'Old Quad'.

On to the pavement again at the east end of Princes Street for a restaurant nearby. After both had enjoyed a substantial meal and, as with people in accord there could be eloquent silences, Robert, noticing a faraway look in June's eye, said, 'You're thinking about the criminal cameraman.'

June smiled. 'I was just wondering if we're making too much of overhearing such a brief conversation.'

'No, I don't think so – not when the older one of the two mentioned the money. Anyway, let's try and forget them for the present and sample the theatrical efforts of the Festival Fringe. I'm on my own tomorrow and you're concert-going with your aunt, so what else can I do but look forward to Friday morning, and you.'

As Robert arrived at his lone 'digs' on Wednesday night he had decided to play detective on his own. He was not going to do the sensible thing and inform the Police of what they had heard; firstly, because he was determined June should not get involved, and secondly, for fear of making a fool of himself. How would he explain being up in the NO ADMISSION balcony? The main reason, if only he'd admit it to himself was the natural desire to 'show off' to the girl.

He spent a good part of Thursday at Calton Hill hoping for a return visit by the red Herald and its camera crew, but no luck. He would have liked to mooch around the area of Broughton Street and the Square where June's aunt lived, but didn't like the idea of that formidable, although likeable lady, meeting him somewhere there and he appearing as some love-sick swain unable to keep away from the part of the town where his new girlfriend lived.

With 9.30 sharp on Friday morning at the Usher Hall to look forward to, he eventually got to sleep.

Chapter 5

Robert, too early for his meeting, found that she was even earlier.

June's eyes were bright with excitement. 'I've found them, Robert, I've found the car! The man's name is Prendiss, he's living near us I think, they're going to the Canongate this morning at eleven to a place called Charlie's or something. I was up early, couldn't sleep, had a walk before breakfast, struck lucky at the second garage.'

Before he could speak, she was off again. 'A young lad was just opening the garage gates, I asked had they a red Herald. They had. I hinted that the owner was a suspicious character and could he keep my enquiry a secret and he said anything you say, miss. I asked if he knew where they were staying, he didn't, but guessed it couldn't be far away and added that they were collecting the car this morning at eleven o'clock to pick up something at Charlie's in the Canongate.'

'How did he know that last bit?' cut in Robert when June stopped for breath.

'Because he was working behind another car and overheard the talk, smart lad, I wanted to ask more but a mechanic arrived, so I just said remember it's a secret, and the lad gave me a wink.'

Feeling that his intended detective act was being taken over and not much liking the wink business, Robert at least had the grace to say, 'Oh, well done, June.' Then in an attempt to resume the major role in this investigation, he suggested, 'Let's cancel the Royal Mile where we got to at Deacon Brodie's Tavern and go down to the gardens now and have an early elevenses. Then we could go up to the Mound, down Market Street and round Jeffrey Street to where the Canongate begins and we can get there in plenty of time.'

'To find Charlie's?' said June.

Robert nodded.

In the Canongate, they were now approaching a likely looking character near the Tolbooth clock, standing at his shop door with 'gossip' written all over the bright-eyed face of him.

'Charlie's? Och aye, even the bairns ca' him that,' said this very promising informant. 'Aye, even the bairns, though they're feared for him, ever since he set up a wee burglar alarm affair, hame-made and it nearly blew the breeks aff one o' them climbin' on tae the windae sill at Charlie's back wa' . . . aye, he's an instrument maker o' some sort ah think.'

Their man of many words then went on, 'Och ah've never been able tae see what goes on in that wee workshop o' his – foreigner of course, and yet a Heilant gentleman comes visitin' him regular – a fine figure o' a man. They say this Heilander was his commandin' officer in the war and he set Charlie up in business here after it, because this Charlie, he's Polish they say, once saved the gentleman's life – so they say. That's his shop wi' the black shutters. Was you wantin' him about anything special?'

'Thanks,' said Robert, 'just wanted to know where he was, a friend of ours heard he was a great hand at the clock repairing.'

The young couple smiled their thanks and crossed the road down to the shop where black shutters flanked dusty glass panes.

Robert tried the door handle then June noticed the card in

the window marked CLOSED stuck into the rim of a mechanical doll's hat. They looked into the gloomy interior.

'A shadow,' whispered June, 'I saw a shadow move . . .'

'Let's walk down Holyrood way, don't want to act suspicious, we'll do an about turn after we look in a few shop windows like proper tourists.'

After what seemed like half an hour, although the Canongate Tolbooth clock had moved only seven minutes to show five minutes to eleven, Robert and June were back in the vicinity of their new friend's shop, but far enough away to pretend not to see him still standing at his shop door.

Suddenly Robert in a voice charged with excitement, said, 'Here she comes! Don't look around, just let's walk slowly up. Can you see Charlie's doorway reflected in this shop window? Aye, well let's just watch.'

The red Herald swung into a stop. Prendiss came out of the car and into the 'closed' shop whose door opened as he approached it.

For too long, until Robert's patience was about to give out and he had the rash thought of crossing the road and barging into the shop, at last Prendiss reappeared clutching a large black camera case of the old-fashioned type which he passed to his assistant.

Then with a roar the red car sped down the Canongate and disappeared from sight.

'There go our clues,' breathed Robert, 'one motor containing two probable crooks and a black case, all gone. I'm going to across to see this Charlie.'

'Only if I come with you.'

As they crossed the road, the mechanical doll in the window slowly raised one if its arms brushing the notice stuck in its hat. The notice slowly slid to the base of the window, nothing else moved.

Robert gripped the handle of the mysterious Charlie's door and turned it.

Locked.

He gave the door handle a shake. The doll slowly keeled over on its side.

'Here's our gossip coming down the road,' whispered June.

'Don't want to see *him* – let's get moving,' and they pretended not to hear some undistinguishable query shouted after them, heading for Holyrood at a pace out of keeping with the warmth of the day until they were in sight of the towers of that Palace.

They went into the restaurant of the Abbey Strand for coffee.

'I'll take you round Holyrood, have lunch back here, and then, June, you'll have to try and contact your garage friend soon and see if he knows anything further on these camera crooks' moves.'

Crossing the forecourt of the Palace, Robert drew June's attention to the fountain. 'There's three faces with only four eyes between them all picked out in white against the dark stone carvings, but it will take too long to find them today.'

To pinpoint such a detail would in any event be difficult, with the fountain encircled with a bank of grass decorated with reclining figures, human ones, young tourists, tired.

The Palace was too crowded for their liking and they were soon at the exit door leading in to the ruined aisles of the Abbey of the Holy Rood. The stone paving seemed to cool the summer air and for some time the young pair were alone.

June said, 'Remember I told you I knew something about Holyrood that even you might not know? Did you know that the composer Mendelssohn visited here?'

'No, didn't even know he ever came to Scotland.'

'It's news for you then, Robert, that in his diary of his tour, on arriving in Edinburgh, he came to Holyrood and as he walked these aisles here, the opening phrase of what was to be his Scottish Symphony came into his mind – it goes like this,' and June sang that opening phrase, reminiscent of 'Old unhappy far off things and battles long ago'.

'I have a tape of the symphony at home,' she said.

'Sing that bit again.'

She did, smiling a little self-consciously.

Robert, looking with heightened respect at this girl, said, 'You have just sung the same phrase of music in the same place where Mendelssohn first thought of it . . . I think this is an incident that's kind of special. I don't think I'll ever forget this.'

'Nor will I.'

A small silence. A boy and a girl together and alone standing in the nave of the Chapel Royal the only part of the Abbey Church remaining.

The spell was broken by tourists emerging from the Palace.

The two walked slowly out into the everyday world again.

During lunch at the Abbey Strand, Robert eventually got round to mundane detective business. 'Your aunt expects you back mid-afternoon, doesn't she? Then I'll meet you again at seven for the Lyceum and you can let me know then if you have any further news from your garage boy, if he's around. If not, the show-down whatever it is, isn't 'til next Thursday, so time is on our side.' All that said with more conviction than he really felt.

They took the bus up the Royal Mile where Robert still had some unfinished business in his role as unconventional guide to Edinburgh, but that would keep for another time.

Chapter 6

Friday, twenty minutes to midnight. Robert Hart stood in a shadowed doorway not far from where June was staying. Half an hour before he had left her at her aunt's front door and waved to her as he turned the corner, apparently homeward bound, but when he was out of sight, he began a circular move through the quiet district to come back on his tracks and station himself on watch after checking the garage door in question that no red Herald was there.

The reason for this present vigil was that June had seen her young associate again and been told that the Herald, after leaving that morning (which they knew), was not due back until late, Prendiss having been reminded by the lad's boss that the garage door closed at midnight. At seven minutes to that hour the red car appeared and drove in out of sight.

A few minutes more and Prendiss appeared, his assistant carrying the old camera case slung by its strap over his shoulder. They walked across the road, turned right and vanished.

Robert moved quietly to the corner and began following them into one of the less distinguished looking streets of the New Town, now partially commercialised.

He quickened his pace, taking from his pocket with a jingling flourish, his keys, as he noticed a rather worn sign Guest House, in the offing. He prayed that this was their destination.

He was now only a few paces behind the two.

Prendiss, hearing the footsteps, turned to look, but Robert was apparently concentrating on disentangling one of his keys.

The two went up the steps to the guest house front door.

Robert, relieved that so far all was well, followed, and as Prendiss produced a latch key, Robert said, 'Good evening, and well met – this key's a bit temperamental at times.'

Prendiss grunted.

Robert followed them in, closing the door quietly behind him, immediately feeling an almost irresistible impulse to open it again and run at high speed as far as possible away from all this involvement, but he steeled himself to continue into the hallway and when they walked along the ground floor corridor he began walking up the stairs to the upper floor.

A door at the end of this upper floor corridor had a sign in metal lettering with the 'I' missing. It read 'TO-LET'. Robert opened that door, entered and locked it from the inside, hoping that in the now all pervading uncanny silence no one in that building would hear the thumping of his heart. And now what? All his moves had been entirely unrehearsed, and more of a similar nature were to follow.

After some ten minutes which seemed to the young man in the small room to be an hour, there was the sound of a door opening in the corridor below, then the opening and shutting of a door immediately beneath him.

Robert could hardly stand the inaction much longer. The house was still quiet except for the recent door noises from below. He slipped off his shoes and stuck them into the pockets of his jacket, pulled the old-fashioned chain of the cistern and in the resultant noise moved along the corridor and downstairs for a step or two until he could see through the bannister railings to the ground floor below.

Crouching low, he concentrated his attention on a bedroom door which had been left ajar, disclosing in the brighter light within the bedroom what he assumed must be the head and shoulders of Prendiss at that moment turning grumpily away from the light, pulling the sheets around him.

Robert now played his part in a series of inspired moves.

Walking silently downstairs with the feeling that his hair was beginning to stand on end, he stopped at the partly opened doorway and put a finger and thumb to the face of the Yale-type lock, then withdrew his fingers carefully, walked back upstairs to his observation post and waited.

A noise of water flushing and taps gushing and then a pause. Like a shuffling zombie, Syd came along the corridor, pushed the bedroom door open and pushed it shut with a click – the 'click' coming from the door handle. Syd in his tired state had naturally not noticed that since leaving the bedroom, the all important inside catch that locked the door had been pushed by Robert into the unlocked position.

A strip of light showed under the bedroom door, then vanished.

So far, that action had kept down the tension but now there was nothing to do but wait. There was one awful moment when the front door opened, softly shut, and muffled footsteps went down into the basement.

Wait ... wait ... and when Robert could stand the suspense no longer he crept down and stood listening at the bedroom door. A musical snoring ... Prendiss? And what about Syd? A chance had to be taken and Robert ready for a fight, but praying that Syd was also asleep, slowly turned the handle of the door, opened it and paused ... He slipped through into the bedroom and pushed the door to the near closed position and stood very still ... the snoring was now subdued. No sound from what was presumably the position of the other bed.

When his eyes became accustomed to the gloom, the only illumination coming from a nearby street lamp, he saw the humped form of Prendiss, now snoring in a different key, and at the other side of the room, Syd, face to the wall and deathly still. Robert had been ready for a proper set to, before fleeing the house confident that he'd have the best of any fight with a half-wakened opponent. He took a small torch from his inside pocket and knelt down on the well-worn carpet, shining the thin beam round the room.

There it was, the black case almost hidden beside an untidy chairful of clothes. He crawled across the carpet and eased the case out away from the bed. This was IT. If he managed to open the case – and he put out of his mind the possibility of explosive. The torch again, it showed a small button on the side but no usual clasp on the front of the case lid. With the sweat coming out of his body, he pressed the button. The lid rose smoothly and silently.

Although what he saw were the obvious contents, an old fashioned whole-plate camera of brass and mahogany upended and closed, fitting in with a series of slides, the whole snugly enclosed in faded green baize, he felt sick with disappointment. He pocketed his torch and about to press the button, presumably to close the lid, when his fingers touched a small wheel. Out came the torch again. He turned the wheel experimentally.

It was no camera! The lid of the case had remained in its opened position, but what had looked like the side of a camera and slides inside, had, with the operating of the wheel, silently risen, being no more than about an inch thick – the top surface of the lid a masterpiece of mahogany and brass made to look like the surface of a camera and slides edged in green baize.

This extra lid in its upright position, revealed the real contents of the case.

What it contained under this false lid had him staring in disbelief. He even forgot for a moment his dangerous situation.

Why *that*? Then he thought, this is that Charlie's work. With his mind racing, he closed both lids, crawled across with the case to its former position, crawled to the door, softly closed it from the outside, opened the front door and out into the clean fresh night air, feeling he'd now like to let out a yell of relief and delight at having successfully found what it was all about.

As the blood pounded in his head he thought, just wait, just wait till I tell June what I've found!

As he hurried along the quiet street homeward bound, he was oblivious to the glance of a late night strolling couple amused at the sight of a young man, his frowning face lost in thought, as yet unaware that he still had the heel of a shoe sticking out of each outside pocket as he swiftly paced the pavement in his stockinged feet.

Chapter 7

Saturday morning.
Robert Hart, suffering from lack of sleep, had June Ralston worried. He was a different lad from the one she had said goodnight to the previous evening.

They had been together this morning for about twenty minutes and he had responded to her attempts at getting some conversation going by answering in brief vague sentences.

Miss Ralston was beginning to feel a fit of huffiness coming on as they paced slowly up the path above the railway line in Princes Street Gardens. They were on the topmost path leading to the esplanade, when Robert, as they neared one of the garden seats, said, 'Sit down a minutes, June.'

'Why? Are you tired?'

'No, no, listen please,' Robert looked around in an almost comic fashion to ensure they were alone, then said, 'That Prendiss, I think he's going to try and steal the Scottish Crown!'

June sat down.

Robert joined her.

She said, 'The one we saw in the Castle on Monday?'

'That's the one. I have an old copy of the London magazine *The Sphere* illustrating the scene when the Crown was carried before the Queen when she attended a Service of Dedication in St Giles' not long after her Coronation.'

Few visitors were using the path at that hour of the day and Robert had the chance to launch into a full account of his adventure of Friday night and early Saturday morning. 'And there I was,' he concluded, 'staring into the big case in that pair's bedroom – and beautifully padded under the double lid – a replica of the Scottish Crown.'

'What would they be doing with a replica?'

'You may well ask – I think they are going to do a switch.'

'A switch? You mean they're going to pinch the Crown and leave this fake in its place. I can't see how.'

'Nor can I – although I have a glimmer of an idea, but can't explain, except that at some point the officials in attendance must be going to have their attention distracted in some way – how, I really don't know. Anyway, it's going to take nerve. I remember Prendiss said something when they were in Nelson's Column, about if it didn't come off they'd play it straight; meaning, I suppose that they would actually photograph the real Crown and the scheme would fall through.'

'But why,' said June, 'should they want to steal *that*? I mean they didn't look as if they would know what to do with it and how did they get permission?'

'Och, I've been thinking of that, well – that and you,' and he smiled for the first time that day. 'This is what I reckon: they're in the pay of some fanatic who is giving them enough to make the risk worthwhile. Prendiss gave the impression that he's an old-fashioned photographer who has seen better days and for some reason is losing business to the up and coming younger lot. He must have written permission to take the photographs and it all fits in, for Thursday night is the Tattoo lads' night off and there will be peace to go up to the Castle and take shots without anyone else around except some officials. And that Charlie in the Canongate,' Robert went on, 'I'm sure he made the replica for there's plenty of detailed illustration in the official brochure on sale, even a diagram of the setting of the jewels. I bet he was up there as a tourist more than once – and for sure Charlie made the fake camera top.

'Here's another guess,' said Robert now in full flow, 'when we saw them collect the case in the Canongate they were gone all that day from the garage and arrived back late last night – what's the betting that they were off to the Highland gentleman that gossip at his shop door told us about? And that it's this Highlander who covets the Crown and they were visiting him for final instructions – or am I way off beam?'

'Oh, I don't know,' frowned June, 'sounds as if you were trying out a plot for a story. Do you think you should go to the Police now or even the Military?'

'No, I will not have you involved.'

'But I want to be.'

'No.' They looked steadily at each other . . . the stirrings of their first row?

Smoothing over the threatening situation, he said, 'All right. On Thursday we'll both go up to the Castle after it's closed and ask to see the guard commander, telling him just enough, no mention of Crowns, to persuade him when Prendiss appears to have the car searched as we think that he's a suspicious character. Then I can guess the reaction to that of the average guard commander, it will be *us* who are the suspicious characters. Och June, let's try and forget it for a while, let's do our best to finish the Royal Mile today and try to enjoy ourselves, eh?'

'Yes,' said June, knowing well that this lad would be scheming before Thursday to form a plan where he could act the hero. 'Yes, we'll do just that Robert,' and gave him a special smile.

'Good. Then let's up to the esplanade and down the Mile, first stop St Giles.'

* * *

They sat in St Giles quiet interior near where the four great Norman pillars supported the 'Crown Imperial' steeple. The quietness was induced simply by the fact that the doors had not long been open to the public for the day and the tourist influx had not yet got into its stride.

Robert said, 'There's historic times when this kirk has been anything but quiet, just as in wars, religious differences sparked off the trouble, when women in the congregation hurled their stools at the pulpit objecting to having "Mass said at their lug". And another volume of noise more in keeping, would be when John Knox was preaching here, a man very strong in his views it might be said.' Robert then asked June to look down beside her feet. 'See that plaque with "JK" on the metal? June looked down and said, 'Yes, why is it there?'

'It used to be in Parliament Square behind the kirk – it marks the grave of John Knox. Where Parliament Square is now, used to be an ancient burial ground and I should think that when it became a car park – the burial ground I mean – in modern times, it was thought by the authorities not right that the great man's resting place should have the memorial plaque sometimes under the wheels of a motor car.'

Changing the subject, Robert said, 'One morning coming up the High Street, two girls with hiker packs on their backs asked me the way to the Castle. They were obviously strangers for if there hadn't been a fairly thick morning mist – we call it a "haar" – they would have seen it from where they stood which was just outside the kirk here. I explained that if they went up to the Castle at that time, there would be no views to be seen, but the mist should clear in about an hour, meantime I could show them the entrance to Parliament Hall behind St Giles. I took them through the door of the Court of Session at the south west corner of the Square and left them at the entrance into the Hall, once the seat of Scotland's Parliament before the Union of England in 1707.'

Robert, who had been on advertising business in that November morning of the previous year, had not then the time to show the girls around the Hall.

He described to June how he still could remember the expressions on the young hikers faces at such a sight, of the great hammer-beam roof glowing in the amber lighting, causing an 'other-world' effect with a haze of the morning mist having crept in above the bewigged and gowned men of the Law pacing the Hall while waiting the call to their various Courts, the whole, making a picture of eighteenth century Edinburgh come alive again.

As they left St Giles, the quarters bells boomed out solemnly from the belfry above, housing not only the quarters, but the hour bell which, although since recast, is the same bell that tolled following the tragic news of the battle of Flodden.

Robert remarked as they crossed to Parliament Hall, 'The hour bell never strikes now, at least as far as I know. I'd reason to ask last year for a friend of mine who had wanted to record the sound, why it no longer struck the hour, and the firm who look after all the City clocks, yes, same place where that lad works who talked to us in Nelson's Column, told me that the ancient hammer which struck the bell had been broken and was in fact downstairs in their workshop. I wonder if it's still there?'

After Parliament Hall which duly impressed, they walked across Parliament Square, passing the equestrian statue of Charles II on his leaden horse. Following the Restoration of the Monarchy and Charles' occupying the throne, a quick change of effigy had been effected, for the originally intended horseman was to have been Oliver Cromwell in his role as Lord Protector of Scotland.

Before they joined the Royal Mile again where the old Mercat

Cross is emblazoned in the heraldry of the Scottish Burghs, Robert turned June round for another look at Parliament Square and said, 'That's another place that was not always so quiet as it is now.'

Robert was referring to the time when, just before the Union of the Scottish and English Parliaments, the notorious Edinburgh mob of the Old Town were in action in the Square.

The mob, very much against the Union, hammered on the doors of the Hall, attacked the exterior walls – the old building vulnerable then, before the Georgian façade was introduced – yelling for the Lord Chancellor's blood, or that of any other of the notables concerned in the final discussions on the Union, to the extent that eventually the Treaty had to be signed elsewhere. The Lords scuttled off by a rear entrance at night and signatures were applied to the all important document in a cellar in the High Street opposite the Tron Kirk, the signing completed later in a garden at Moray House in the Canongate.

One further note on that historic time: in these early days of the eighteenth century there was still a stand of music bells on the roof of the belfry of St Giles next door, on which on week days melodies from popular songs of the period were played to charm the ears of those in the busy confines of the Royal Mile below.

On the day of the Union one wonders who chose to feature the tune of a favourite of the time, its title; *'How Can I Be Sad on my Wedding Day.'*

June and Robert were now into their final tour of the Royal Mile. Down they went to where the North and South Bridges bisected the High Street by the Tron Kirk steeple, its former steeple having been a victim of the Great Fire of the 1820s. Here was a reminder that once the 'tron' itself, a weighing machine, was handy for having some offenders of the Law nailed by their ears to the beam in punishment. The site was also the gathering place of the citizens, as it still is, to 'Bring in the New Year'. On to the Museum of Childhood opposite John Knox's house and a few yards down and on the same side of the street, Robert pointed to a stone carving high on one of the tenement walls.

'That's a model of the Netherbow Port, the gateway once here,' and he took her down to the end of the High Street and showed her the brass plates set into the causeway, marking where the Port's position was in the town wall.

'Edinburgh once ended here,' added Robert, 'the rest of the way to Holyrood being the Burgh of the Canongate.'

When Prince Charlie and his men arrived from the west they did not come into the Royal Mile but wheeled round to Holyrood Park and to the Palace to steer clear of the Castle battery of cannon as they were at that time unsure of the kind of reception expected. Cameron of Lochiel, a staunch supporter of the Prince's Cause, chose to try his luck with his Cameron men that night and, going north from the Park, came up by the east facing town wall and to the vicinity of the Netherbow Port. With drawn swords the Camerons waited. Lochiel grasped the opportunity to advance as the Port gateway was open to allow passage through of a coach into the Canongate then, pinning the gatekeeper to the wall he signalled to his men. In that way Edinburgh Town was 'taken' while most of her citizens were asleep, and taken without bloodshed.

Now into the Canongate, less commercialised than the High Street section of the Royal Mile and with good restoration of the façades of the houses, which although modernised inside, present a face to the street of the eighteenth century revived.

An especially good example is Chessel's Court which Robert pointed out as the setting for Deacon Brodie's final burglary.

'Oh, the Tavern man?' asked June.

'The same,' said Robert, 'but let's go into this cafe. It seems quiet, too early for the elevenses lot and I'll give you the tale, at least part of it, for a pal of mine showed me the typescript of a story he had written on the Deacon, and he's trying to find a publisher. I think I said to you when we first discussed him, that Brodie deserved a book about his extraordinary life.

'Deacon William Brodie was a respected member of the community and concerned with Town Council business, and not the first man to lead a double life, for he was a burglar at night. And not only that, he kept two mistresses, one in a house in the High Street and the other near that Tavern we were in, in a part now vanished when the George IV Bridge was constructed. He had five children by these women and looking after his two families and being a terrible man for gambling, but not too fortunate at that, meant that apart from his successful and lawful carpenters business, he never had enough money. So, dressed in black and masked, he prowled the streets and closes and wynds at night, with his 'dark' lantern and a bunch of keys at the ready.

'During proper business calls, he managed often by distracting the owner, to take the man's keys from its nail on the inside of the front door – a traditional practice then throughout the town. He would choose one to press into the wee box of putty he kept in his pocket, before returning it to the nail. This impression he'd take to a blacksmith whom he was blackmailing, to have a phoney key made.

'Brodie was very successful as long as he worked solo. Then he met three men of the same crooked kind at the cockfights in the Grassmarket and at the card tables in the drinking howffs and so the Brodie gang came into being.

'This criminal quartet did very well at first. They even stole the silver mace of the University of Edinburgh and sent it by coach to their fence in England to be melted down. Their ambitions reached a peak on deciding to rob the Excise Office, at that time in the 1790s, housed in Chessel's Court. The plan for the robbery was well worked out: one man at the front door on watch, another outside to warn by prearranged whistle of the approach of any authority and two inside for the job. In the darkness however, a mistaken identity situation, solely due to the return of a member of the staff to collect some papers, created a farcical situation and their venture failed.

'In time, by a series of unlucky coincidences for the gang, three were arrested with Brodie still free, but, although honour among thieves has been occasionally known, Brodie was not taking any risks, guessing that one of his former associates, on the chance of being granted a pardon, might squeal on the Deacon. Brodie fled the town. He got to London and crossed to the Continent where he actually wrote to a friend in Edinburgh asking him to be ready to send on his carpenters tools to New York, for it was his aim to begin a new life in America. He nearly got away with it, but was recognised at one of the Channel ports and arrested and escorted back to Edinburgh.'

June said, 'What a man! Did he get a long prison sentence?'

'He was hanged. Hanged on a scaffold near where that Heart of Midlothian stone heart is on the causeway by St Giles. "It would be a leap in the dark," Brodie had remarked when he heard the sentence and the only time he showed any emotion was when his favourite daughter Cecilia came to see him in the Tolbooth prison by St Giles.

'He even arranged that, after the hanging, his body should be quickly put on to a barrow by his own workmen and run up Castlehill in the hope that the rough roadway might revive him and bring him back to life – but that was one plan of his without success.'

Out again to the Canongate and the bright morning washed away any dark thoughts on Deacon Brodie as they approached another Tolbooth, the Canongate Tolbooth with its clock case decorated with the Canongate heraldic arms of a cross between a stag's antlers, commemorating the legend of how David I of Scotland, when out hunting, was confronted by a giant stag coming in for the kill. As the king prayed for help, so a vision of a cross appeared before the beast who backed away and vanished into the forest.

In gratitude for the deliverance, David caused the Abbey of the Holy Rood, or Cross, to be built.

Today, adjoining the Tolbooth, the Canongate Kirk is now the Royal place of worship to succeed the ruined Abbey. The front row of the kirk pews shows the heraldic arms of the reigning sovereign with others of the Royal House.

Continuing down a few steps from the kirk and on the same side of Dunbar's Close, was one of the surprises of this Mile of surprises, a formal garden laid out in the manner of the seventeenth century. Here June and Robert stayed for a while, having the arboured pleasure to themselves and a consequent genuine absence for some minutes of any thoughts of what the coming Thursday might bring.

Later, as the towers of the Palace hove in sight, Robert asked, 'Lunch?' and when they were seated, said, 'That's definitely the end of my official guide act June, I sure had to study as I've never done for years to get the information for the firm's brochure – we tried to get away from a lot of the usual guide book stuff. Now can we plan at least a couple of days beyond the City and go roving, and climb Caerketton?'

'Yes, but this afternoon,' smiled June, 'let's climb Arthur's Seat.'

Chapter 8

Other characters associated with this story were also climbing, but with a complete absence of enthusiasm.

Prendiss and Syd had indeed gone to see the mysterious coveter of the Crown but had been invited, no, commanded, to return for a few days in the bracing Highland air and so to induce an extra fitness and thus a keen alertness for the coming job.

The criminal pair were never likely to forget these few days, not only for the climbing, but the walking through heather-toughened moorland which was a nightmare for both.

The only reward so far as Prendiss was concerned, the opportunity of a record of the view from Craigower Hill looking west, the prospect of the Pass of Tummel leading the eye to the peak of Schiehallion above the Tummel loch and on to Rannoch with the Three Sisters of Glencoe on the horizon.

Said their host, 'The Road to the Isles, what? The song, by Tummel and Loch Rannoch and Lochaber I will go, Glencoe in Lochaber, see?'

No, they didn't see.

How glad they were to get back to their slightly sleazy 'digs' in Edinburgh. They brought back with them the very necessary permit for entry to the Castle, in the form of a letter from an American illustrated magazine whose editor had already written to the authorities concerning permission to photograph, which had been granted. That the editor in the

USA was ignorant of all such transactions is explained by their host having a loyal friend on the editorial staff of the magazine, also a fanatical Jacobite, only too willing to arrange forgeries for the 'Cause', he being close to the editor in the matter of correspondence, and a trusted secretary, knowledgeable about Scotland and useful in vetting or advising the editor when contributions from Scottish readers and writers had to be considered.

June and Robert had a much better time. They had agreed on two ventures beyond the City confines before the fatal evening of the coming Thursday. Robert suggested hiring a car, being a driver but not an owner. June said the one snag about that was always having to come back to where the car had been left.

'Let's take bus runs,' suggested the girl.

They took a bus to Hillend then walked west below where the Pentland hills were scarred with the longest artificial ski slopes in Europe, until they arrived at Swanston village and indeed climbed 'Steep Caerketton', following in the footsteps of RLS.

From that high top they continued west then downhill and so to the village of Colinton where a bus took them back to town. That was on the Monday.

On Wednesday a special jaunt. They boarded a bus to South Queensferry beside the Rail and Road Bridges over the Forth, then walked the shoreside woodland path back to Dalmeny House. Here, among many other attractions, was a life-size bronze of a former Earl of Rosebery's Derby winner, statuesque before the entrance door. Within was the Earl's collection of personal possessions of Napoleon. The house had an air of welcome and of animation, of pleasant coming and going, explained when they were told that the present Lady Rosebery and her husband the Earl were friends both of attenders at the

Festival and personalities of stage and concert platform taking part in this famed international event.

That special day was completed when, after continuing through the woods to the Cramond shore, the ferry boat took them across the mouth of the river Almond to Cramond Inn, the village the site of a Roman camp, the Inn marking this with its sign above the door of a Roman soldier.

Chapter 9

Agreement with the three concerned, (Miss Macower being ignorant of the criminal camera goings on of the other two), that Sunday and Tuesday would be for June and her aunt, meant that on these days Robert had time on his own for detective work.

He spent the admission fee into the Castle more than once, with attention concentrated in the Crown Room. Here it should be explained that the present comparatively recent innovation of the impressive story of the Crown as illustrated in the series of rooms in Crown Square, was not what Robert saw. This story takes place in the early 1990s when the Crown Room was indeed but one room with the complete Regalia as the centre piece of a single display.

He might also have been seen more than once, studying the lower walls of the Argyll Tower from below where the garden path opens out into a kind of platform flanked on one side by railings.

It had happened that one day a year or two previously, leaving his office for a short-cut up the garden paths to the esplanade and so to the library in George IV Bridge, he had noticed a group of youths also heading up the slope and finishing under the wall at the Argyll Tower. He was about to turn his attention to the gate leading into the esplanade when two of the youths began climbing on the part of the rock below the Tower wall. Robert did an about turn and told the party that going into the Castle that way was asking for trouble. One of the group, they were German students, was told to call them down. One did reappear and come down but the other vanished until his head was seen framed on high through foliage. There was an exchange between the one on high and the leader of the group down below, then the head vanished. As far as Robert could understand, for his informant spoke good English, the one above was stuck. Time passed, perhaps no more than ten minutes, when unbelievably the rogue climber appeared at the gate into the gardens on the Mound roadway below! He joined the party in a considerable sweat and Robert, not wishing to become involved in any official reaction to this informal entry into the fortress, departed the scene very quickly.

Robert had never understood how the German boy had managed to drop down to the cobbled way inside the Castle, then speed down to the exit at the drawbridge, cross the esplanade and, not noticing the little gate at the corner into the garden slope, find his way down Ramsay Lane to the Mound and the garden entrance there.*

Now Robert, inspecting that part of the wall by the Argyll Tower, noticed that the bush that had hidden the climber that day had since been removed disclosing a heavy cable, probably a power cable, attached horizontally to the stone wall. This could be used as a hold, thought Robert, when working along to reach the wall where it left the higher part of the Tower and it would become possible to climb over and slide down by the big leaden pipe which he knew was on the other side and would land the intruder in to the Castle interior.

---

*Such a climb into the Castle from the garden path below was actually witnessed by the author; also the return of the German youth to his friends. This episode happened some years ago at the height of a tourist season and apparently without any official interference!

Unknown to June, this was his second plan should the guard commander refuse to co-operate. That this alternative was risky he well knew, but the showman side of his nature hoped that he would be in action there on Thursday evening.

June, on another pre-breakfast walk past the garage had been told by her teenage informant that the red car was leaving for good around eight o'clock that evening and this information was phoned from an outside call box to Robert at a time arranged when he would be at his lodging on Thursday forenoon, also the time and place for their meeting that fateful night.

Chapter 10

The day of the grand finale of their adventure dawned on a morning no longer bright with promise but with a sullen high sky of a grey-sulphurous nature. It had been a difficult day for both of them and both were relieved as the evening drew close when action at last – of a kind about which they were not sure, was promised.

Miss Euphemia Macower sat reading in her sitting room that Thursday morning, or at least she had a book before her. Miss Macower was thinking about June, about her preoccupied manner when they had been out together and how her niece had kept out of her way even this morning and gone to meet the young man outside later, as apparently her intention was to do so again this evening.

Miss Macower dismissed the thought that there was an elopement in the offing. Too soon. Far too soon, even allowing for the fast working of the young ones of today.

So, to the evening, with Miss Macower reading again, at least with that same book before her. There was a mystery in the air as well as a thundery indication that the long sunny spell was about to end.

She heard June's footsteps approaching, the girl looked round the door of the sitting-room. 'Goodnight, auntie, don't wait up, we're going to one of the late-night shows.'

'Goodnight dear,' smiled Miss Macower.

Immediately the outside door was closed, the aunt dumped

the book, grabbed her waterproof coat, an old tweed hat and from the hall stand, a hefty walking stick.

Before June was at the end of the Square, Miss Macower, in the earlier than usual dim light brought on by an overcast sky, was on her trail.

The aunt had in her time read many thrillers where suspects were shadowed with ease, but she found the reality of trying to do so rather different.

She stopped in a doorway to watch the meeting of the young couple.

Shadowing them was difficult in Leith Street, a lesser woman would have panicked when twice she lost them, and the east end of Princes Street with a crossing at the lights there, complicated the business all the more.

The going was easier when the young pair turned down into Waverley Bridge although their trailer would have wished for a less eager pace shown by the quarry, particularly when they turned right and, passing the Festival offices, headed up the long brae of Market Street to the Mound, crossing there, on up Mound Place. Here again people in plenty, coming and going by the entrance to the Assembly Halls for the evening theatre performance there.

Miss Macower really lost them this time and temporarily at least, gave up the chase for a well earned breather.

She resumed the steep way up Ramsay Lane and on to Castlehill. She looked down Castlehill. No one. She looked up to the head of Castlehill. No one.

Miss Macower, a lone figure under the Tattoo banners of Scottish Command hung from on high, arrived at the entrance to the esplanade and looked down the stairway of Castle Wynd North. A cat, a black shadow, crossed the steps but nothing else moved.

She walked on to the esplanade, feeling that all her efforts had gone for nothing, her sudden mood of gloom matched the eerie emptiness of the dark area before her. The Castle floodlighting not yet being switched on meant that only two lights were apparent: one from the brazier fire of the nightwatchman's on the south east corner of the stands for the Tattoo and the other from the smaller door of the drawbridge entrance. Against that light two figures were silhouetted which Miss Macower thought she recognised as June and Robert.

She settled down at a corner of the stands to await developments, her mood of disappointment suddenly changed to a subdued excitement. That young couple hadn't come all this way to visit the Castle at night when it was closed except for a very good reason – if it *was* them.

Robert, surprised that there was no sentry in the box at the drawbridge, and feeling slightly daft, thumped a double-knock for the second time on the Castle door.

Studded boots sounded across the pavement inside, the smaller door set into the main entrance doorway opened. Robert said, 'I wish to speak to the guard commander please.'

'What aboot, sir?' said the small but stocky kilted one, eyeing June with favour.

'Private and official business.'

'Jist a minute.' The kilted one was replaced in the doorway by a taller version with two stripes on his arm who said politely but warily, 'Can I help you?'

'Yes, I've reason to believe that a photographer is coming here shortly to the Castle and I've information which I think means the car should be searched before he gets any further than this entrance.'

'What kind of information?'

'Sorry, the less people know about this the better, all I ask is that you—'

'Now lissen, son,' broke in the corporal, lapsing from his official English to his native tongue, 'maybe there's a photographer comin', although how you ken this beats me, and maybe I've got papers to prove identity and permission for to—'

'They'll be fakes I tell you. All I ask is that you should search the car. Please listen and—'

'Naw, YOU listen,' the guard commander took his eyes off June and looked directly at Robert. 'You ken what? Ah'll bet you're one o' thae students up tae some bloomin' stupid stunt fur capturin' the Castle, an' when the car *diz* arrive, bet there's mair o' ye'll suddenly appear. Have ye tipped off a press photographer tae be on the scene?' That impressive speech by the corporal showed imagination of a high order and suggested that he had already suffered from 'thae bloody students' in his military career.

'Off you go son, an' if it wisna' that there wiz a lady present, ah'd tell you *where* tae go – or wid ye prefer tae be arrested?'

Robert turned to June, 'Come on, it's no use here.'

As they walked down the esplanade, a disappointed girl said, 'You gave up easily, Robert.'

'Not given up. It's hopeless there, I thought it might be. I've got an alternative plan.'

Robert, a bit nervous about this alternative as the reality of what he was about to attempt sunk in, was at the same time secretly pleased, for this other way had much more glamour, the chance to show off to his new girl?

As they left the esplanade, he said, 'I'm going in another way. Believe me it's OK. You must trust me.'

'Only if I go with you.'

'This time, no. This is a little climbing job that I've gone over. I've actually seen it done in daylight, honest, it's safe and you must go home please, and wait—'

'This time, no!' They stopped and faced each other.

'Well,' sighed Robert, 'will you go back and stay near the nightwatchman on the esplanade? Talk to him about his job, anything. Tell him you're waiting for someone to come out of the Castle which happens to be true. I really won't be long according to the times you found out about.'

'All right, I'll stay by the watchman, but it'll be horrible with me there and you doing a climb out of sight.'

He refused further details of his scheme as they returned down Ramsay Lane and round to the garden gate on the Mound slope where they stood near the lamp standard by the gate and, when there were no walkers in the vicinity, he gripped the base of the ornate spikes on top of the railing and drew himself up, then got a steadying hold on the ornate standard before twisting round to ease down to the other side of the stone base of the railings.

'Won't be long, June,' and he turned to go, but June said, 'Robert.' He faced about again. She stood on tiptoe on the stonework at the base of the railings.

She kissed him and gripped his shoulders almost fiercely, saying, 'Please be careful – I'd hate if anything happened to you now.'

Robert said nothing and disappeared into the dusk of the garden slopes, all set now to fight dragons if need be, let alone criminal cameramen.

As Robert disappeared in the direction of the Castle rock, June, feeling very much alone, walked back among the Assembly Hall's arrivals and was confronted by an elderly lady at the entrance to Ramsay Garden.

Said the elderly lady, 'Well miss, and what have you to say for yourself and where has Robert gone?'

'Auntie! What are you doing here? How did you get to—?'

'*I'm* asking the questions, June, come now, what's it all about, eh?'

'*Please* come back to the esplanade Auntie, please come back there first.'

Miss Macower, noticing the anxious expression on her niece's face, said, 'Very well, we'll go up to the esplanade. We'll tell the watchman that my officer nephew is coming out from the Castle shortly on leave and we're here to surprise him—' Here, June interrupted saying with a slight hysterical giggle, 'There's more than that maybe coming out of the Castle soon to surprise us.'

The aunt looked concerned. Not like the girl to be in such a nervous state. Sympathy for her young charge took the place of the annoyance of being kept in the dark by the young couple and she said more gently, 'All right my dear, we'll go up now and see the watchman, then sit somewhere out of earshot of the man and you'll tell me all about it.'

Robert's route did not require any crossing of the grassy slopes. He found his way on the earthen path leading up to where it broadened out like a platform under the rock thrust out as if supporting the Argyll Tower above.

His eyes had gradually become accustomed to the gloom contrasting with the glitter of Princes Street and the lighting from the Gardens bandstand below where an orchestra was playing a carefree melody for the couples on the dance floor there.

Robert, feeling anything but carefree, began the climb.

Heaving himself on to the initial footholds was as difficult, so far as mountaineering was concerned, as anything he met further up, and very soon he realised two truths: that the climb must be more difficult at night than in the daytime and that his suit, especially the trousers, was now ruined.

At long last on to a verge of grass under the wall and above, the welcome handhold of the thick power cable to support him along to where the gable of the Argyll Tower gave way to the lower wall lining the roadway. At that moment two events happened – the Castle floodlighting came on and a car was heard driving slowly up from the Castle entrance. Almost certainly Prendiss, according to information Robert had been given for the photographer's arrival.

The length of time between Robert reaching that lower wall and his planned arrival in Crown Square was to take longer than had the climb, for, apart from the floodlighting making the problem of concealing his movements that much more difficult, it seemed that following the arrival of that car he had heard, the place had become alive with the sound of marching boots and more vehicles – a sound track he could well have done without, for now another anxiety arose to trouble him: what if he couldn't get to Crown Square before Prendiss had performed his trick and vanished?

At last, silence around the Castle. He looked over the wall. No one in sight. Taking a deep breath, he swung himself over to the roadway side and, feeling very exposed as his floodlit person momentarily cast his giant shadow on the Argyll Tower façade, went down by the big leaden pipe and was under the archway and through to the foot of the Lang Stairs up which he went at a stumbling speed, praying that he wouldn't meet anyone coming down.

Crouched at the head of the stairs, he waited until he recovered his breath for the next move.

There was a mutter of thunder behind lowering cloud and it was a measure of the tension he was suffering that he jerked nervously when the first big raindrop spat on to his outstretched hand. Then he was running across to where the entrance to Crown Square was flanked on his right by the Scottish National War Memorial and on his left by the historic apartments containing the Crown Room.

The Square was deserted. The rain, destined to be a brief shower, was making up for this by coming down in earnest. Robert ran for the shelter of a car – yes, it was the red Herald, the only vehicle in the Square. He hid behind it as he considered how best to approach the room formerly visited by him as a 'tourist' more than once in recent days.

The increasing darkness was relieved only by a moderate glow of light showing from the doorway leading up to the Crown Room.

He heard a burst of laughter coming from that doorway. Prendiss making some joke? What a nerve the man must have, considering the situation, thought Robert.

From the shelter of the car he reappeared, a shadow among shadows, a lone rain-soaked, trouser-torn, muddied, knee-bloodied figure moving soundlessly to the entrance to the Crown Room. Slowly he crept up the short flight of stairs to lower himself full length on the steps and all hidden in shadow, so that his head was on a level with the floor of the Crown Room.*

Beside the showcase containing the Regalia stood presumably, the Keeper of these 'Honours of Scotland', and one other official. Prendiss was bent over his equipment and Syd stood by, all this seen through the heavy metal grill across the opening leading to the Crown Room. Both this grill and the weighty door accompanying it would normally be closed when the Crown Room was not available to visitors, but the door itself had been swung back against the side wall because of the airless heat of the evening.

---

*It should be noted that this adventure is placed in the early 1990s just before the Crown and the rest of the Regalia became the nucleus of a much more extensive display taking up extra space on this east side of the Square.

The Crown had been taken from its usual display position and now rested on a small velvet-draped dais no more than a few inches from the floor.

'Now for the close-up looking down view the magazine particularly asked for.'

And Prendiss contracted the legs of the camera stand and focused . . . 'I'd like some light reflecting on the shadowed side. Bring over the spare camera Sydney. We'll place it so . . . and open the lid.'

The big black camera case was now on the floor beside the small dais supporting the Crown, its open lid apparently showing the side and accompanying slides of a camera of the old type in mahogany and brass.

'Now,' said Prendiss, 'something white to put into the inside of the open lid to reflect the flashlight on to the shadowed side.' He took a letter from his inner pocket and pressed the white sheet of paper into the inside of the lid. 'A bit of improvisation, gentlemen. Sydney, just keep the white page in that position with your finger tips and keep it steady until I get the shot.'

The photographer then picked up a basin-shaped shade with a battery connected to a powerful electric bulb in the centre and surrounded by a mosaic of small mirrors and turning to the two officials remarked, 'I know I'm old fashioned in the way I go about my work these days but I've had both these cameras for many years and they still work effectively for me. I think I'll have this patented, gentlemen,' and he indicated the shade he was holding. 'These little mirrors are faceted to concentrate the light – didn't need it for the other shots, but this one of the Crown requires the ultimate depth of focus and my camera does not have the lens depth as do some of these modern idiot-proof ones.'

Prendiss grinned at his own mild joke, but noticing a hint

of impatience in one of the officials went quickly on to say, 'With this light I can stop down to the smallest aperture of the lens.'

With his back to the dais and screening the Crown from the officials' view, he held out the lamp showing the two men the inside and said, *'Note the reflector, gentlemen,'* and a miniature lightning flash filled one half of the room.

Robert, remembering the phrase Prendiss had given as the cue for action instinctively shut his eyes at the all important moment, then saw Syd with nerveless capable hands taking the Crown off the dais, laying it on the floor, raising the inner lid of the black case, taking out the replica Crown and placing it on the dais, inserting the real Crown into the case, closing the inner lid and resuming his hold on the sheet of white paper – all that in thirteen seconds, while mild confusion reigned in the room with Prendiss apologizing profusely, saying that the trigger was much too sensitive and it wasn't the first time that had happened, himself once being temporarily unsighted. The two disgruntled officials gradually began to see again, one of them observing that it was a damned careless thing to do.

'Oh dear, I'm really sorry about that,' said Prendiss for about the fifth time, 'but no harm done eh? And you all right Sydney?'

Syd, kneeling by the black case and wearing glasses temporarily to enhance a professional look, nodded, and for the first time since coming to Edinburgh, smiled.

Prendiss now had to take at least one picture of the fake crown. Robert could not but admire the man's nerve.

Putting himself in the officials' place, Robert thought what would be their reaction if a dishevelled youth with a large tear in his trousers, showing a bloodied knee and with hands and face scratched and blackened by earth and rubble, stood up and shouted through the grill that the cameraman had just stolen the Crown? No, it wouldn't do. For one thing, considering the priceless objects in the room, an alarm system must surely be installed.

As Prendiss produced another flash, on the fake crown this time, Robert was slithering backwards down the short flight of steps and off and running for the guard room, meeting on the way one solitary soldier returning to barracks from leave, observing to the world in general, 'Where there's trouble, it's aye a wummin, so it is.'

Arriving at the guard room door he did not stand on ceremony but shoved it open and staggered in. The guard commander grabbed this apparition, not sure if he was seeing things, then recognised the copper-coloured head all plastered wet on the visitor's brow. 'YOU again, YOU! How the hell did you manage tae—'

'Turn out the guard, *please*, turn out the guard,' gasped Robert. 'Aye, it's me again.'

The guard commander looked steadily at his unexpected caller and then with a surprising expression of sympathy signalled to one of his men to bring a mug of the ever available tea.

The guard themselves sensed a diversion coming to pass the weary hours and it had stopped raining.

Between gulps of tea, Robert finished a brief explanation with, 'I can't tell you what it's all about, but there's a big black case in the photographer's car and there's something in that case which could set off a nationwide sensation and honestly Corporal, I'd hate to be you if this criminal cameraman got away with it – in fact I'm surprised that there hasn't been some kind of explosion before this. He should be appearing any minute.'

In the brief silence that followed, a car could he heard approaching the archway of the Argyll Tower . . . at that the guard commander straightened his belt, adjusted his bonnet, strode to the door and swinging round, bawled, 'GUARD TURN OUT!'

The criminal cameraman's face which had been wearing an expression of gloating triumph as he left Crown Square, changed to one of considerable concern on seeing a line of soldiers with fixed bayonets on the cobbled way.

The Corporal held out a hand. Prendiss opened the side window. 'What's all this about, soldier? We're in something of a hurry y'know.'

'Routine sir, just routine, won't be a minute, got to search the car.'

'But this is nonsense, all we've been concerned with is—'

'Excuse me sir,' cut in the guard commander and signalled to two of his men who lifted the cloth from the car's rear seat and shone a torch on the equipment; then the key for the boot was grudgingly given while Prendiss kept revving the engine impatiently. Nothing unusual in the boot. The Corporal looked murderously at Robert who whispered to him, 'Something in the front seat, the lad's knees look awkwardly high up, could be he's got the case under them.'

At that precise moment a distraction in the form of a loud blare from a motor horn came from the outer side of the drawbridge.

'Jeeze,' said one of the guards reverently, 'the Colonel!' and trotted down to the big doors. Almost before he had both sides opened, the Colonel's car was barging in.

The Colonel, peering through his windscreen, saw a line of his men, a scruffy youth in civvies and a red car. He slowed down and swung clear to the left. Prendiss saw his chance, shooting forward with the soldier who was about to close the Castle doors sent flying back against the wall as the photographer sent the red Herald at lunatic speed for the northeast exit corner of the esplanade, followed by a line of soldiers led by Robert shouting in daft fashion considering the situation, 'Stop the car, June, stop the car!'

It was Miss Macower however, to June's alarm, who went into action as the red car approached, her aunt walking forward as if to meet the Herald, spray flying from its wheels. She stopped and raising her hefty walking stick like a sword of freedom, sent it whirling, by luck it must be admitted, smack against the side window of the car causing Prendiss to jerk the steering wheel in reaction. The surface of the esplanade newly soaked after a long dry spell did the rest, the sudden move on the steering wheel sending the car into a sliding swerve to crash against the railinged wall of Ramsay Garden with Prendiss slumped over the wheel.

Syd, unhurt, was out of the car and climbing up the outer edge of the Tattoo stands with the big case slung by its strap like a knapsack on his back. When he reached the top tier of seats desperation gave him an agility foreign to his nature as he slid and clutched at scaffolding and canvas in a descent on the dark gardens side, dropping down to vanish like a rat into what looked to him like a black void and with the uncomfortable feeling that someone was repeating his scaffolding climb, which was indeed the case – Robert was after him.

Both were now sliding and slipping down the wet grass at speed, Syd handicapped by the weight of his burden and Robert about at the end of his tether physically, seeing Syd periodically as a silhouette against the glow from the Gardens bandstand.

The unlawful bearer of this symbol of the Kingdom of Scotland was unaware that he was travelling in the general direction of the Perthshire Highlands to where if all had gone well for him and the cameraman, the Crown would have been delivered to the Jacobite fanatic who believed himself to be the last of the Royal Stuart line.

Syd stumbled on to the railway bridge, at one and the same time seeing that a wooden gate was fastened across the far end of it and that a bedraggled someone was coming out of the gloom after him.

Syd reached the gate, clambered on to it, but Robert made a flying tackle and both rolled back on to the footway of the bridge.

A struggle in the near darkness then Syd wrenched himself free and dived again for the gate.

Robert almost threw him back on to the footway with what was all but the last of his remaining strength. His opponent aimed a flying kick, which Robert ducked clear under and with shoulders hunched brought all his weight against the raised leg. With a yell of pain Syd described a backward curve, hit his head against the side of the bridge and lay still.

'Here they are!' bawled a now well known voice and a trio of soldiers, one of them the Corporal with a torch, came on to the bridge. Syd, slowly coming to, was roughly jerked to his feet and Robert leaning against the side of the bridge suddenly became unnaturally animated considering his condition and with a high-pitched yell, cried, 'The Cr-, the case, where's the case?' Then in a more normal tone, 'Shine your torch on the railway lines Corporal.'

No sign of anything except the railway lines and some paper litter. Robert turned on Syd and gripping him by the collar, growled, 'The case – where's the case?' Syd, with all the fire knocked out of him, nodded towards the gate.

Robert ran to the gate and looked over. 'It's here, he must have lowered it over the gate by its strap just before I spotted him -can you get one of your men Corporal to get it back – I haven't the strength.'

'Nae bother,' said the guard commander and clambered over

himself. Said Robert, 'For God's sake don't touch any of these brass fittings, hold it by the strap and give it me over the gate. Inside it's cushioned against being thrown about, but there's a small wheel at the side and if it was turned . . . well . . .'

The Corporal with mounting respect for Robert, gingerly handed the case across.

A pre-arranged signal by torch to the esplanade, then a small procession went slowly up the garden paths above the railway. In the rear, Syd, firmly between two kilted figures, in front, Robert clasping the black case, shuffling wearily beside the Corporal who said, 'Sorry about turnin' you away at the drawbridge up there.'

'That's OK, would have done the same in your position.'

'Lissen pal, you a boffin's assistant or something? What's *in* the bloody box anyway – just looks like an auld camera case tae me.'

'Well, as I said up at the guard room,' and Robert stopped for breath and to do a bit of quick thinking, 'what's in the case could have caused a nationwide sensation . . . it would have been better from the crook's point of view if they had managed to have left it in the Castle.'

'Then,' observed the Corporal, seeing himself the centre of barrack room attention later, 'they must never have got the chance of doin' the damage up there as planned and they two blokes are in the pay o' a foreign power and we aw ken whae that might be.'

'That's just about it,' nodded a weary but now smiling Robert.

The re-union, as the procession came through the now opened gate leading the path from the gardens on to the esplanade was quite a social occasion with Miss Macower introducing Robert to the Colonel who expressed his congratulations, with

June, unable to stop smiling with relief, also unable to take her eyes off Robert, and the watchman beaming over all in regard for the evening's happenings which had so brightened his usual nightly vigil by the brazier each lonely Thursday. There was also a 'gallery' of a few spectators at upstairs windows in Ramsay Gardens.

With a fine lack of concern for the upholstery of his car, the Colonel drove bedraggled Robert and the ladies up to Crown Square where the keeper of the Regalia's expression when he was shown the contents of the black case, was a moment to cherish – everyone 'in the know' and particularly the Keeper, having good reason to keep the story to themselves.

Miss Macower then suggested to Robert's protestations and June's delight, that he come back to her flat for a long hot bath and a quick needle and thread job on his trousers before she made up a bed for him in the sofa in her sitting room. Upon this the Colonel did an about-turn with his car and promptly took them there.

Of course there were another four who had been involved. Prendiss was treated in the Castle hospital and when recovered, he and his sorry assistant, also having been resident within, were escorted across the Border and set free – with the hint that Scotland Yard would be keeping an official eye on them. The same applied to Canongate 'Charlie' who left the Royal Mile very suddenly.

Finally, the Colonel who had known the fanatic Jacobite of Perthshire in the happier days when they were both young subalterns, went to see him privately. No prosecution there either.

Friday morning.

Miss Macower's guest refreshed, grateful yet relieved that this unexpected domestic interlude was over, insisted on doing a solo bus run to his lodgings there to have a complete change and to don his best suit. Then at a pre-arranged time he would meet June 'for old times sake' at the Usher Hall front door.

The rest of that Friday was wonderful. They lazed the day away. No history. No long walks. No stories . . .

Saturday evening

The succession of thundery showers had released Edinburgh from the heat-wave and a fresh clear gloaming light hung above the Castle as the Mounted Band of the Household Cavalry led by the old Drum Horse left the arena of the Tattoo.

There was silence for a moment after the applause died away, broken only by the sound of cavalry hooves clattering down Castlehill. The huge spotlights then swung back to the Castle drawbridge . . . beyond could be heard faint wild music gradually becoming louder and louder as both parts of the great door of the Castle opened in unison and into the arena came the Massed Pipes and Drums of the Scottish Regiments, fanning out in strict formation coming down the esplanade in a glitter of shining ornament to the swing of the tartan and the fierce pulsing beat of the drums.

There had been some last minute rearranging to allow four seats to be kept specially in the Royal Box of the stands.

There sat Miss Macower with the Colonel and June with Robert.

As the line of Drum Majors approached the foot of the esplanade Miss Macower glanced sideways at the young couple.

Robert, gallantly scarred a bit about the face, sat solidly looking ahead, the muscles of his jaw working slightly. June's eyes shone bright, the brighter for the hint of tears. Her left hand was firmly, very firmly, clasped in Robert's right. Miss Macower noticed this too and, nodding slightly to herself in satisfaction, turned her eyes again to the brave spectacle before her on the esplanade.

Miss Macower was well content.